Bloodstained Tales Of Sin and Sex

Bloodstained
Tales
Of Sin and Sex

By

DAVID J. HEARNE

Edited by

Michael Garrett
Stephen King's First Editor

SUBTERFUGE
PUBLISHING

Bloodstained Tales of Sin and Sex

Published by Subterfuge Publishing
PO Box 8008
Lumberton, Texas 77657
www.subterfugepublishing.com

Cover Design by:
Victoria Quezada
www.David-Hearne.com

ISBN 978-0-9755976-2-0

Library of Congress Cataloging-in-Publication Data
Is available on request
Printed in the United States of America

To my wife Stacie for her support, tolerance, and love.

Dreams are the roots of reality

ACKNOWLEDGMENTS

It's time to thank some friends and colleagues who were generous with their time, expertise, advice and the always needed encouragement. They all played a role in the completion of Bloodstained Tales of Sin and Sex, directly or indirectly.

I am very grateful to Michael Garrett, Stephen King's First Editor for his editorial support, and advice to help me complete this book of short stories. It is great to work with an editor who has worked with authors like Joyce Carol Oates, Richard Christian Matheson, Brian Lumley, and Nancy A. Collins to name a few.

I also need to thank Yvonne Johnson, a prolific author of over 65 books who got me writing professionally in 1990. Thanks for your trust and confidence in my work.

Finally I need to recognize those associates and friends who inspired me or kept me going: Mike & Karen Fuljenz, Jim King, Jannie Venter, Mayank Vadher, Chris Kyle, Robert & Diane Verde, Elaine Henderson, Megan Moore, Eric Compton, Pamela Truax, Sheila Bailleaux, Callie Hearne, Dennis Hearne, Gary Linthicum and my good friend – that I see too little of, Mark Wulf.

Table of Contents

THE STRANGLER FIG

Fifty feet above me was the outline of the remains of my great grandfather, Willy Taylor, or more affectionately referred to as Great Pa. His outline glistened from the rain, and it looked as if he was staring down on the strange happenings below. The huge Banyan tree swished and shook like it was undergoing a massive electric shock treatment. Even its scraggy aerial roots wavered back and forth in some sort of rapturous excitement.

Muffled by a roll of thunder, a horrible guttural noise bellowed from the naked man standing under the Banyan's thrashing branches. His cries and pleas of mercy would go unanswered, and I'd feel no guilt for the horror that was there awaiting him. That day had been coming for many decades, and I'll remember it as the Taylors' day of atonement.

Back in the early nineteen hundreds, Willy Taylor, my Great Pa, was the best cabinet maker in Key West. Everyone agreed, even Big Jim Dillon, the Klarogo or Sergeant of Arms of the local Ku Klux Klan. If anyone wanted a cabinet or chest made right, they would go to Willy Taylor.

In 1930 my Great Pa had fallen ill and started having dizzy spells. He wasn't really all that old, maybe about forty, so he figured the condition would just pass, but instead, the spells got worse and often he'd pass out right where he stood.

One day in October 1930 Big Jim Dillon sent a message to my Great Pa to come to his house and build him an armoire for his new wife, Thelma. My Great Gram claimed that the new Mrs. Dillon was a bitter white woman as mean as a cornered rattlesnake. Great Gram's warning made no difference to Great Pa since there was no way to say no to a job from a member of the KKK, especially its Sergeant of Arms.

The second day on the job, Mrs. Dillon came in to tell my Great Pa to leave because she had some white ladies coming over, and she didn't want them to see no sweaty black man in her house. While she stood there glaring coldly at him, my Great pa had one of his spells.

As he collapsed, one of his flailing hands accidentally grasped Mrs. Dillon's bodice and ripped it open. When he came to, a group of astonished white women were all looking down at him, but even worse, he saw that Mrs. Dillon was crying and grasping her torn bodice. As Great Pa shakily rose from the floor, Thelma cursed and shrieked at him that he'd pay mighty when Big Jim heard about this.

Great Pa didn't have to wait long to see what awaited him. Later that very evening some unwelcomed visitors banged on his front door yelling, "Open the door, coon." When he finally opened the door, six hooded and robed KKK members burst into the house and pummeled Great Pa to the floor. The hooded men said they had a big lesson of respect to teach him about white women; at least that's what they claimed they were there for.

My Great Gram was there and watched everything that happened. In fact, she had no choice because they made her watch. They even made fourteen-year-old Shirley watch as they beat her father. Great Gram knew who they were and right off recognized the gravelly voice of Big Jim Dillon. He was the most violent of all the KKK men there that night. Dillon had brought with him a sledge hammer, and after they all finished kicking and punching my Great Pa, they pinned him to the floor. My Great Gram told me she begged them not to do what she knew they were about to do. She tried to cover him with her body, but they just tossed her aside, then they did it anyway.

Big Jim Dillon raised the sledge hammer over his head and smashed it down on Great Pa's right hand. All its bones splintered into hundreds of fragments, some even sticking out of the mangled mess. The hand was now nothing but an unrecognizable mound of red pulp twitching at the end of his wrist and oozing with blood. While he yelled in excruciating pain, Dillon moved over to Great Pa's left hand. He raised the sledgehammer once more and slammed it down hard destroying Great Pa's other hand. Bones protruded from the red mounds of flesh, and Great Pa shrieked in agony. Great Gram yelled at them and told them enough, but Dillon wasn't finished. He came over to where Great Gram and Shirley stood and punched Great Gram in the face and told her to shut her mouth and show respect. Dillon grabbed Shirley, pulled her over to the kitchen table, and bent her over its edge. He pulled Shirley's skirt up over her back and started raping her in front of everyone. Great Pa had been pulled up from the floor by a couple KKK members and was told to watch his little bitch get it. Suddenly, Dillon was grunting like some hog with a sow, and his hood started falling off his head, but he didn't take no notice.

No one was really holding my Great Pa any longer; he just stood there with his mangled hands dripping blood on the floor. Unexpectedly, he took a couple steps forward, then suddenly pounced onto Dillon's back and bit deep into his exposed neck. He bit so hard that when he pulled back, a large chunk of Dillon's flesh filled Great Pa's mouth. Before Dillon could react, Great Pa buried his teeth again. This time he ripped off most of Dillon's left ear and spat it onto the floor. Dillon was yelling, shrieking, and begging the others to get that goddamn crazy nigger off him.

When they pulled Great Pa off, the unmasked rapist was so shocked that he just stood there with his pants down around his ankles exposing his dangling shrinking appendage to all. When he realized that his left ear was gone and a bunch of flesh was missing from his neck, he became enraged.

Hobbled by his pants bunched around his feet, he shuffled to his sledge hammer leaning against the kitchen wall. He shouted to the men holding Great Pa to bring that coon over to him. When Great Pa stood before him, Dillon smashed the sledge hammer into Great Pa's chest with all his might. The blow was so strong that the head of the hammer embedded into Great Pa's chest. Dillon wiggled it free, leaving a chest grotesquely smashed in on one side. The blow probably killed Great Pa, or knocked him unconscious, because he fell to the floor and never moved again.

After all of that, Great Gram said they pulled Great Pa's body outdoors and hoisted it up into the Banyan tree. They placed his body in one of the tree's crotches where a jumble of branches came together. A large chain secured Great Pa to a huge branch within the cluster, then they just left him there to rot. He's still there, but now he's a part of the tree, a part of its spirit, maybe even its heart and soul.

When the KKK members poured back into the house, Dillon told my Great Gram that she had to leave the house and the Keys in 24 hours and never come back. If she didn't, he told Great Gram that he would hang her and Shirley next from the Banyan tree. He gave her thirty-seven dollars and told her she'd have to sign over the house. She realized she had no choice, so she signed the bill of sale he gave to her.

After they killed Great Pa, Shirley just sat on the floor in a trance with her blood-spotted skirt pulled tight over her knees. She was struggling with this horrible feeling that it was her cries while she was being raped that caused her father to be murdered. Did she cry out to her father to save her? She couldn't remember, but she felt she had. Her heart was broken. She'd loved her father and was so proud of him, and a part of her was glad he did attack this monster who had raped her. She knew her father must have really loved her to have just used his teeth to stop that bastard from raping her. She wondered if the others would have taken turns with her if her dad hadn't done what he did.

Something white and bloody under the kitchen table caught her attention; it was Dillon's ear, and suddenly she knew she had to have it. When the KKK men left her alone, she crawled over to the table and snatched it up.

Dillon's ear was all pretty much in one piece, complete with stubbles of blond hair protruding out of it. She quickly shoved it into the pocket of her skirt and crawled back to the wall.

Great Gram walked about the house in a daze collecting the few possessions they could fit in the valise the white men had given them to carry away their belongings. She had over a hundred dollars saved up that she hid in her under-garments and a couple gold coins she stuck in her shoes. She hoped the white men wouldn't search her and take what lit-tle money they had.

When morning came, the white men told them it was time to leave. The twenty-four hours weren't up, but there was nothing left to do, so Great Gram and Shirley stepped out into the bright October morning and started walking down the dusty road to their new life.

About a month after they murdered Great Pa, the Dillons moved into the house. The house was much grander than Dillon's former home, and he wanted to show it off a bit. Everyone was awed by the beautiful home, its woodwork and its beautiful landscaping that my Great Pa had worked so hard to perfect.

The center piece of the front lawn was the massive Ban-yan tree. It towered above the house shading it from the hot summer sun and sheltering it from the gale force winds that often swept in from the ocean. Great Gram said that Great Pa would bury dead fish all around the tree to help it grow. He loved the tree and would sit under it often and read his books and make his plans for the next day. He told Great Gram that he could think clearer when he was under the Banyan's huge canopy.

Great Pa had become friends with an Indian man; not an American Indian, but a man who came straight from India. The man's name was Mayank, and he was some sort of spiritual leader for the few Hindus who lived in the Keys. He told Great Pa that the Banyan tree wasn't like other trees, but a tree that could live forever and had many powers that helped humans.

"The great Buddha achieved his enlightenment sitting under the Banyan tree, and the leaf of the tree is the resting place for the God Krishna," Mayank told Great Pa.

It could also fulfill wishes if you believed strong enough in its powers and prayed to it. The holy man, Mayank, often brought ancient Sanskrit books and read them to Great Pa. They told of the many spirits that dwelled within the Banyan tree. Most important he told Great Pa that if you provoke those spirits, great harm, illness, misfortune, and death will be your fate. When the Banyan spirits are angry, it becomes the strangling fig to those who offend it.

Shirley had swung from a swing that Great Pa had hung from a branch of the Banyan tree. She spent many afternoons swinging in the tree and often was observed talking to it. Great Gram told her if people caught her talking to it, they'd think she was crazy, but Shirley just kept chatting to it anyway. She told Great Pa that sometimes she felt the big Banyan tree would wiggle its branch and her swing would magically move back and forth without even pumping her legs. Great Pa said she was just imagining it, but she swore it was real. She loved it as much as her father and fed it food like he had.

When Shirley left their home and passed under the Banyan tree that last time, she made a fervent wish that it would kill the men who killed her father and stole their home. In her hand she squeezed the severed ear as she made her silent appeal.

Three weeks after Dillon had moved into Taylor's home, he decided to trim some of the branches from the Banyan tree. When he swung his axe at one of its branches, a huge swarm of wasps flew out of a hive high above. They circled him like some small tornado, then suddenly covered him like a black blanket of pain. They crawled up under his shirt and up his pant legs. Nothing was sacred to them. He tried to cry out but they entered his mouth stinging his tongue, lips, and gums. Their buzz sounded like the roar of a jet engine. They stung him over and over until he was just a bloated mass of bites. When his wife, Thelma, found him an hour later, the wasps were gone and only his swollen purple body lay there with his mouth locked in a grotesque grimace of horror. It was even more hideous because he'd bitten off his tongue during the attack. While she stood there looking down at her dead husband, the Banyan's aerial roots swung to and fro as if possessed and taunting the bereaved Thelma.

Six months after Big Jim Dillon's death, Thelma gave birth to a son, Paul Dillon. Without Jim being around, things were tough, so Thelma invited her departed husband's eighteen year old sister, Celeste, to move in to help make things easier for both of them.

Celeste loved living in Key West and quickly met a young man named Stanly, who was a sailor stationed at the naval air station. Soon he was staying over at her house, and she fell deeply in love with him. Things were getting much better financially also due to his contribution to the household. About a year after they had met, Celeste started having female issues, and to her dismay and shame, discovered she had a bad case of gonorrhea.

In the nineteen-thirties, treatment was iffy for something like gonorrhea, and many doctors had no idea how to treat a woman, but Celeste was lucky because she lived in a navy town where being infected with gonorrhea was like a sailor's rite of passage, and treatment was readily available.

Celeste started an expensive treatment of anti-gonococcal-vaccines, and a couple months later she was free of the drips, a lot poorer, and very single.

During this same period my Great Gram and Shirley had settled in Beaver Dam, TX, a small shanty town where Great Gram had family. They moved in with Great Gram's sister, Inez, and helped on their small farm.

A few months after arriving, Shirley realized that she was pregnant. She wanted to rid herself of the thing growing inside her, a horrible living reminder of the man who had killed her father and created so much grief for their family, but Great Gram said no. She was afraid that anything they might do could hurt Shirley and she couldn't bear to lose her only child after all she'd endured.

Later that year a baby girl was born and, to their utter shock, the baby was almost totally white. Great Gram named the baby girl Rosie because it had such red cheeks.

Shirley felt nothing but hate and anger for her baby girl and wanted nothing to do with it. She wanted to drop it off at some orphanage, but Great Gram wouldn't hear of that either. Finally, eight years later, her feelings mellowed, and she began to feel pity for Rosie. She came to accept that Rosie wasn't to blame for what had happened, but was simply some strange doings of God's unfathomable plan for her.

When Rosie was eighteen she was such a beautiful woman that every man who saw her lusted after her. She had a hard time in romance because mixed marriages were illegal, and no one could tell that she was supposed to be black. Trying to date a black man meant being harassed for dating out of her race, but dating a white man meant telling him she was really black.

Rosie joined the WACS, and finally in 1956 Corporal Rosie married a Frenchman while stationed in France. They had a baby girl in 1958 whom they named Tillie, and she became my mother in 1980.

My mother said she lived her life as a white person because she was so white, but her birth certificate claimed she was black, so much of her school years had been spent in black schools.

Back in Key West, young Paul Dillon was enjoying his adolescence with his best friend Dusty. They had been friends since kindergarten. Dusty liked to catch iguanas, and some very large ones lived in the Banyan tree in Paul's front lawn. One hot summer afternoon Dusty came over to Dillon's home and, finding him not home, decided to trap one of the iguanas by himself. He hid behind a bush waiting for this two foot long iguana to climb down from the Banyan tree. Dusty had concocted a delicious iguana salad to lure it into his trap. The salad was a mixture of mustard greens, spinach, carrots, peas, zucchini, mangos and other yummy fruits.

While Dusty sat there in hiding, Mrs. Dillon came out on the porch and started yelling for Paul. While she was yelling, the large iguana lumbered down the tree and over to Dusty's pile of iguana bait. Mrs. Dillon spotted the nasty lizard and came running over to chase it away, but tripped over a big Banyan root, falling flat on her face. She sat up and started cursing the tree and its ugly roots, then the oddest thing happened.

According to thirteen-year-old Dusty, the aerial roots started frantically swinging back and forth, then the entire tree shook itself. There wasn't any wind to mention at that time of the day, but the entire giant tree shook as if hit by the winds of a hurricane. She started to back away when a fat aerial root dropped quickly behind her and seemed to en-circle her, then Dusty said he saw this huge snake wrapping itself around her, and it all happened just like magic.

Dusty told the police that it just came from nowhere, and it looked like the boa constrictor he'd seen in a Tarzan mov-ie. Later he told the police that the aerial root itself had just turned into the snake.

Whatever it was, it wrapped itself around her and started to squeeze everything out of her. The first thing that ush-ered from her mouth was a terrifying scream that slowly ebbed to just a shuttering sound, then nothing as the snake's coils contracted tighter and tighter, squeezing every molecule of air from her lungs.

Dusty told the police he saw every minute of what hap-pened. He said the snake first pulled her to the ground and, as she struggled, the snake's head would just hover over her face as she desperately fought for air. The bulbous snake's head, with its gleaming yellow eyes, tipped back and forth, inquisitively studying the struggling Mrs. Dillon. It seemed to leer at her as her eyes began to bulge from their sockets. Spittle dripped from her gaping mouth, then her tongue suddenly protruded from it as the snake's coils rippled with an even tighter deadly embrace. A couple times it darted its scaly head toward her face; it opened its mouth wide, showing its elongated fangs glistening with drops of mucous. The snake's nose would widen as its pointed tongue darted toward Mrs. Dillon's tortured face. It would emit an unworldly hiss, then pull its head back and return to studying its human prey as another ripple of sinews tightened its coils even tighter around Mrs. Dillon.

The snake was so powerful that blood and vomit gushed out of Paul's mother's mouth. The snake coils stayed still for a few moments, then another ripple went through them and the coils constricted even tighter. Her tan shorts began to turn dark from the excrement squeezed from her bowels.

Dusty told the police that all the time the snake was squishing the guts out of Mrs. Dillon, the snake just continued staring into her blood-covered face. Finally, its coils relaxed and it unwound itself from Mrs. Dillon's still body. It slithered up to the Banyan tree and disappeared.

Dusty told the police it was the tree that killed her, that the Banyan tree had powers or something, but the sheriff told the hysteric Dusty that the shock of seeing a snake kill a woman had made him see things that he really hadn't. Dusty didn't argue, but he never came by the Banyan tree again because he knew that this tree could kill and it would again if it wanted to.

The loss of his mother was hard on Paul, but he struggled on. By his seventeenth birthday, Paul was six feet tall. He had a job as a carpenter's helper that gave him the exercise and exposure to the sun that hardened his muscles and tanned his body.

Celeste was proud of her nephew's good looks and his talents with tools at such a young age. She wanted to help him grow into a real man and started talking to him about getting a girlfriend, but she also began to feel a tinge of anguish when she thought of him leaving her. She'd stayed chaste since her experience with her cheating sailor and her gonorrhea infection, but now seeing Paul's glistening muscles and broad chest, a strange feeling enveloped her. She felt the need to be touched again. It was an overpowering feeling that she couldn't shake.

She started devising innocent ways for her handsome Paul to touch her. She complained about how sore her muscles were from all the housework and the raking up of the large Banyan leaves that blanketed their yard.

His touch felt good, very good. He had wonderful hands. As time went by, Celeste graduated to having Paul rub lotion on her many sore muscles and, once totally relaxed, she'd dismiss him from her room.

Paul would often linger outside his aunt's bedroom door and listen to the squeaking of her bed as she relieved her tormenting tickle. Some nights it was just the opposite; Celeste would listen to Paul's bed creaking in that rhythmic fashion of someone taking matters into their own hand. The squeaks and lustful moans would inflame her, and soon her fingers were soothing herself in a similar fashion.

One winter evening, hearing the sporadic gasps emanating from Paul's bedroom and feeling the warmth spreading through her loins, Celeste suddenly realized her responsibility. She went to Paul's door and hesitantly knocked on it. She tried the handle, but it was locked. Paul came to the door and let her in. She told him they had to talk about some issues that just couldn't wait any longer. Celeste smiled at Paul and said she'd been shirking her duties as his guardian and needed to address some things that a father would normally have taken care of.

She sat on the side of his bed basking in his muskiness. She felt a wetness spread to her thighs as she said, "Paul, we need to talk about sex. I know it'll feel awkward and a bit embarrassing, but you're a grown man and it's time you learn about women and how to please them."

Celeste looked at her frightened nephew and said, "I know you've never knew of me having a man, but I once did. It was when you were just a little boy. I know what it's like to feel that sexy feeling and wish there was someone to love you. I certainly went through all that when I was your age, but you have to be careful. I'm going to tell you a secret about myself. I had sex with a man I thought I loved when I was young and much to my humiliation; I ended up with a bad disease because he was unfaithful. He'd slept with all kinds of filthy girls. I'd never want this to happen to you. But you still need to learn about sex so you won't be embarrassed when you find that special person you might want to spend your life with. I want to teach you some of those things because I love you."

Paul was mute and stared blankly at his aunt's face. Celeste grabbed his hand and caressed her breast with it. She told him that this was something all women love. She pressed his fingers to her hard nipples and watched his eyes widen. She felt the tremble in Paul's hand, and his excitement aroused her even more. She stood next to his bed, shook off her robe, and pushed his hand down over her belly until it touched her wetness. Fifteen minutes later the virgin Paul was history. Celeste pecked some loving kisses on his cheek and told her shaken nephew that their exciting adventure had to stay a secret, but hoped he'd want to learn more on another night.

The winter of 1971 was a joyous one for Paul and Celeste, but in late April of 1972 Celeste found herself suddenly gaining weight and realized that the curse had also abandoned her. When she finally told Paul that they would soon have their own love child, he panicked and went to a Santeria priestess named Lilly who knew all kinds of spells. He'd heard she could cast spells so powerful that they could change the course of a hurricane.

He wanted the child to die in his aunt's womb. Lilly told him that was possible, but for her to help, he must tell her all he'd done to upset the gods and be prepared to pay highly for her intervention.

He gave Lilly almost six hundred dollars and told her the entire titillating tale of sexual union with his aunt, but Celeste's sins were unforgivable, and even Lilly's strong magic couldn't prevent the birth of their darling baby boy. Celeste named the baby Wayne after the actor John Wayne.

To say the least, things around home weren't the same any longer. The baby had put a damper on the steamy romance the two had shared. They argued and fumed, and when he'd stay out all night, she'd feel both anger and seething jealousy as she pictured him between the loins of another woman.

A month after baby Wayne was born, Paul paid a return visit to Lilly's house of magic and demanded a refund. Lilly said no, and the next day she found herself staring up at a hospital ceiling. Lilly swore to herself to get revenge on Paul.

Two days later, Lilly returned to her home. Her house was in total disarray, and she soon discovered that all her money was gone except a single dollar bill which displayed a message reading, "I wiped my ass with this one, so you can keep it." She called upon all the Santeria gods to help with her revenge.

Things were up and down for many years between Paul and his aunt, but now Paul had a sense something major was wrong between them. She just didn't seem to care for her handsome nephew like she once did. She hadn't visited him in the night for months. Of course, it was a lot more difficult now that Wayne was eighteen; their boy was pretty observant. Paul had grown to feel proud of his son even though he never could claim him as his own.

Things had soured in this very loving family and the lack of love from Auntie bothered Paul. He needed to find time to give her more attention. One sunny afternoon the bulldozer Paul drove blew a pressure line. While the mechanic worked on it, Paul decided to slip home and try to rekindle the dying embers that had brightly burned for so long.

On his way home he stopped at a florist and bought a bouquet of roses for his sweet aunt. He couldn't remember which color she liked, so he bought a mixture. He knew he couldn't go wrong with a mixture. The remainder of the drive home he fantasized about the ensuing intimacy he'd have with his beautiful aunt.

When he entered the house, Celeste wasn't prone on the couch in front of the TV as she normally would be. He thought she must be taking a nap. He quietly snuck down the hall and stood outside her door. Inside he could hear what sounded like Celeste watching a torrid love story or some porno flick on the TV. She had the sound really cranked up. The anticipation mixed with the guttural sounds of copulating humans had him burning with desire as he swung open the door to Celeste's boudoir. He held the bouquet of roses in front of his bulging trousers as he stepped through the threshold. To his amazement, the TV was off, but the sounds of passion still filled the room.

The sounds were coming from a jumble of arms and legs all intertwined in the middle of her king-size bed. He quickly recognized Auntie's sexy legs bent back so far that her knees touched her shoulders. Between Celeste's shapely legs was the pistoning posterior of mommy's big boy.

The grunts and moans of ecstasy filled the steamy room like the vulgarity and cacophony of rap. The noise sounded as loud as the roar of a crowd witnessing the last touchdown in a Super Bowl game.

Paul's stomach clenched, as he moved to the side of Celeste's bed and saw his son suckling on her teats. Her eyes were rolled back in her head as she shouted encouragement, "That's it, sweetie, that's it, make mommy happy."

Paul seemed to be invisible to both of them. Then suddenly his rage exploded and he whipped the beautiful bouquet of roses across Celeste's lipstick-smeared face.

Celeste shrieked, "Holy Christ!" as her eyes fluttered open. She recognized Paul's face glaring down at her and instantly unlocked her strappy high heel-clad feet from around her son's waist.

Wayne shot up off his mother as if a bomb had exploded between them. He was out of his mother's boudoir in a second flat.

Paul, still enraged over his two-timing aunt, levied a string of epitaphs against her. "You fucking whore," spewed from his mouth, followed by an explosion of other curses and threats. His stomach was so upset now that he was sure he'd vomit and, if he did' he'd projectile it on Celeste. He could smell her cheap perfume, sweat, and the musky odor of fresh sex.

Paul stood there for another moment and yelled, "I'm leaving and never coming back."

Celeste's eyes filled with tears, but Paul stomped out of the room and marched to his car cursing every step of the way. He heard the clomping of her heels behind him. As she hurried to catch up with him, she yelled, "I was just trying to help him like I did for you. Don't leave me. We're family. I love you." Her words burned into his ears as he slid into the driver's seat. Before he could start the car, the passenger door flew opened and a naked Celeste dove in. Her breasts heaved as she begged him to stay. "I'm sorry!" she repeated over and over. Paul didn't answer. He revved the motor, threw the car into gear, and raced straight across the weed-laden lawn, ripping small aerial roots out of the earth. Suddenly the car was airborne.

A huge limb of the Banyan tree held the car in its grip and was now moving it out over the road in front of their home. It held the car high up in its green foliage. For the moment, Paul and Celeste forgot about her dalliance with their son and they reached out to each other for support. The car hung precariously from the branch, and Paul and Celeste fell from their seats onto the front windshield. They tried not to break it because they were afraid they would then fall out. The car swung back and forth, and Paul tried to figure out what had happened, but before the answer came, the Banyan tree shook violently, parted its branches below them, and released the car. Like a one ton missile, the car fell eighty feet, smashing into the asphalt below. A second later, an eighteen wheeler rolled over it, crushing it almost flat. The mangled mess burst into flames, and somewhere deep within the tangled mess Aunt Celeste and her nephew Paul roasted.

I was nineteen when my mother told me the story of Great Pa and Great Gram and showed me the shriveled ear that once was a part of Dillon's face. Later that year I took a trip to Key West to see the old home and what had happened to the bastards who had blighted my great grandparents' life, and with me was the ear.

When I first saw the old home, I was shocked because it looked nothing like I had imagined. It was a rundown house in terrible shape. Shutters hung from rusted hinges, roof shingles were missing, and the yard was a tangle of weeds.

Crushed and mud covered beer cans littered the ground around the front porch. Juxtaposed to all this ugliness stood the majestic beautiful Banyan tree. Its branches with their large green leaves covered it like a living umbrella.

The Banyan tree seemed to draw me closer to its center, to this large trunk that had lived over a hundred years. I worried that someone inside the house would see me and want to know why I was on their property, but the tree held more power over me. I found myself standing next to the enormous tree trunk, and I reached out and stroked it. It felt warm, and my fingers sort of tingled as I stroked it. Suddenly something touched the back of my neck and I froze in fear. It was one of the aerial roots. It moved up and down my neck, tousled my hair, then pulled its woody member away from me.

I felt this strange feeling of warmth surge through me, and a total feeling of calm embraced me. Oddly, a flood of tears poured down my face, but not from fear or sorrow, but from some well of love that electrified my being. Now three of these aerial roots appeared to caress and stroke me. One gnarly root lifted my chin so I was looking high up into its branches, and mysteriously, a mass of branches parted, displaying something that my eyes couldn't believe.

A tapestry of roots held a skeleton of a man against its trunk. In fact, it looked like the skeleton had been grafted into the large Banyan's trunk. I knew without doubt that the skeleton was my Great Pa's remains. I also realized that the two were now one. My Great Pa was now part of the Banyan's powerful spirit, part of its heart. My communion with the Banyan tree was suddenly interrupted by a scraggly looking man standing on the porch shouting at me.

"Get the hell off my property. This ain't no tourist attraction," he yelled.

I quickly moved away from the tree and, as I did, it visually vibrated and flung its aerial roots around in a total frenzy. It's sort of crazy, but I think it was upset that I was leaving.
I didn't know who the man was on the porch, but soon discovered it was Celeste Dillon's grown boy, Wayne.

I had come to Key West to avenge my ancestors, and now, after meeting Wayne Dillon and seeing my family's old home, I knew revenge was my duty, but what would this revenge be? Even the Banyan tree seemed to welcome me back, and I swore I wouldn't fail this calling.

I got a job washing dishes at a Key West tourist trap and found a cheap room not far from where the old home was. Every day I'd walk by the old home, and the Banyan tree seemed to reach out to me. In fact, every time I neared it, my entire being would experience these little electrical tingles. Every time I went by, some of its aerial roots would swing out toward me, then the entire tree mass would quiver.

I quickly found myself falling in love with Key West. It was so alive, so much to do. One evening as I was prowling the streets, I came across Lilly's House of Magic and felt this strong urge to enter. The old woman inside looked strangely at me and said, "I'm Lilly, welcome to my botanica. I provide all the spiritual, religious, and mystical needs for Santeria, voodoo, occult, and pagan rituals. How can I help you?"

I told her I was just looking and suddenly she clasped my hand resting on the counter. A look of awe filled her face, which then turned to a knowing smile.

She apologized for touching me, but said that her touch revealed more to her about her visitors than their words. I replied, "So tell me then, why am I here?"

She looked straight into my eyes and said, "You're here for revenge, to right a horrible injustice that started many years ago. You're here to fulfill destiny; to kill someone."

Her answer scared me because it was something that had entered my mind, and I had experienced recurring dreams where I'd introduce myself to Wayne as his black cousin, then shoot him in the face or stab him in his heart. Mostly I'd dream of hanging him from the Banyan tree, but that was just unconscious dreaming; I couldn't really do something like that. I wasn't a violent person.

Lilly said, "You'll need the help of La Santa Muerte, The Holy Dead, to avoid man's law. You'll need my help." Her matter-of-factness alarmed me. How could she know something I had never told anyone?

I said to her, "You really do have a great imagination, but this time you're way off. Why would you say these things to me?"

She replied, "I'm a Santeria priestess; an old Santeria priestess who has guided Santeria followers for many years. The truth can't hide from me. I see people's thoughts and secrets in splashes of colors, in auras, and I've seen yours many times because they're the same as..."

She paused, as if in deep thought, then, looking knowingly into my eyes said, "The same colored patterns as mine. We share a death wish for the same person, a Mr. Wayne Dillon."

She paused again to let what she'd said sink in, then told

her story of her earlier encounter with Wayne's father. My doubt vanished. She knew my thoughts. I didn't tell her what I thought, but of course, she knew it anyway. I left her that evening with the promise that I'd think about her offer.

The next night after work I hurried back to her botanica. She welcomed me and brought me to the back of the store. She told me that the following Tuesday would be a perfect night to perform the black magic necessary to kill Wayne. I asked,"What would I have to do. Would I have to shoot or stab him?"

"No, no!" she replied, "The saints will grant us our wishes. The saints will fulfill his destiny."

"First we must discover your Orisha," Lilly said to me, "Everyone has a ruling Orisha, a deity that looks after you. Once we know yours, you'll have to communicate with him and offer a sacrifice to please him. Even more important you must communicate and pray to Oloddumare, who's the all-powerful, totally transcendent god who rules over all Orishas. You must learn to have faith in your Orisha and Oloddumare.

"For you to gain the cosmic power to perform the magic you'll need to make an offering, an ebbo, to your Orisha. You'll also have to pay me for the magic to work. A Santeria priestess magic won't work if she doesn't receive money from the benefactor of her work. It shows belief in Santeria powers, and belief is a must for our magic to work."

The next few nights were a whirlwind of strange customs. Suddenly Tuesday arrived, and at 5 pm I returned to Lilly's store. In her back room a large group of Santeria believers greeted me. The room was full of activity. Men were beating unusual rhythms on their bataa drums to beckon and communicate with the Orishas. The Santeria adherents were reciting prayers to Olodumare.

I closed my eyes and fervently repeated the sacred words also, "Olodumare, the one who encompasses the entire Cosmos. Olodumare, I pay homage to all the ancestors who sit at your feet now. I praise the creative forces and those who sacrificed their own lives for the continuity of life. I pay homage to the awakening sun, the sunrise. I pay homage to the dying sun, the sunset. I pay homage to all eternity, yesterday, today, and tomorrow. I pay homage to the sun and the moon. I pay homage to Mother Earth."

When the prayer ended, the sound of thunder and the patter of rain added to the cacophony that filled Lilly's back room.

A man came to the center of the room and held a chicken high above his head. More prayers were uttered as Lilly, holding a jewel-encrusted knife, approached the squawking chicken. All the while Santeria disciples danced around the room chanting,

"Ori, please, support me.

Ori, please, bless me.

Ori, please, never turn against me."

As the chants got more frenzied, Lilly reached up to the chicken's neck, and with a flick of her wrist, cut off its head. She held the writhing body above her face so the blood spurting from the beheaded chicken filled her mouth. The blood would feed and please the Orisha who lived within her.

With her red-streaked face dripping from chicken blood, Lilly offered me a silver chalice partially filled with sangria and milk. Reciting another prayer, she squeezed the chicken's neck, squirting warm blood into the silver chalice. She then handed the dead chicken to an aide.

The room was full of strange smells and sounds. Cigar smoke swirled around creating a bluish haze that hung like a fog beneath the ceiling. Lilly kept reciting prayers as she swirled the blood, milk, and wine around in the chalice and finally pushed it toward me. My stomach tightened as I took the chalice. I prayed first that I wouldn't vomit up the offering. Lilly told me the drink would appease and nourish my Orisha. As I drank the concoction laced with fresh chicken blood and listened to the chants and words of the worshippers, I felt that I had gained more powers, more knowledge, and was more attuned to the universe, and as those thoughts filled my being, claps of thunder and streaks of lightning etched across the Key West sky.

Finally, Lilly ended the service and washed the dried blood from her face. She bid goodbye to her worshippers one-by-one and, after the last left, she turned to me and said, "It's time. It's time for us to visit your cousin."

Lilly had a car, and we drove over to the house and parked down the block. The rain was still coming down as we walked down the street to the house. We both stood in front of it for a few moments, and above us the Banyan tree shuddered and shook in what felt like a welcome gesture from it. We walked under its huge canopy and up the rotting steps of the porch. I wondered what would really happen this evening and, even more, what I'd say to Wayne.

The lightning flashed across the sky, illuminating the door and its ancient metal knocker. I grabbed it and banged it down a few times till I heard footsteps coming. The door swung open and a disheveled Wayne stood in front of me. Apparently he didn't recognize me from the previous encounter and asked, "What do you folks need?"

The words that I wondered about before just effortlessly came to me. I said, "Wayne, I'm a distant cousin of yours, and this is my friend Lilly who's showing me around Key West. I just wanted to stop by and meet you before I left the Keys."

The rain had picked up and it was blowing right into the entryway.

Wayne looked curiously at me and said," I don't think I got any living cousins. I'm about all that's left of the family. You must be mistaken. Sorry!"

Lilly said, "I don't think we're wrong. Your mother was Celeste Dillon and her brother was Jim Dillon. Correct?"

"Well, yes. Okay, come in for a minute so we can keep the rain out."

Lilly and I entered the house and closed the door. I thought, *so this is the house where they killed my Great Pa and raped Shirley.*

He asked me again how we were supposed to be related and I said, "Well, it goes back quite a few years. You see, my Great Pa built this house."

Wayne said with a snort, "Well, so there you're wrong. An old black man built this house, so sorry, you just got the wrong Dillon."

"No, Wayne, I don't have it wrong," I said emphatically. "Jim Dillon killed my Great Pa and raped my Gram making us like kissing cousins. I guess he'd be my Great Pa if I really wanted to recognize him in my family tree."

"I don't understand what you're talking about, and I think you've had too much sun. You both should leave," Wayne drawled, pointing to the front door.

From my pocket I pulled out a cellophane envelope with the severed ear and told him to look at it. At first he didn't recognize what it was, then I said, "That's your Great Pa's missing ear. We've had it all these years, and I wanted to return it to his family."

"You're fucking deranged," he snapped back.

He stood silent for a few moments looking at the ear, and then said, "So you're my kin? Guess I need to be more hospitable. Come on into the kitchen and I'll show you some family history you'll never forget." He opened the kitchen door and gestured to us to enter.

As I stepped in, he walked to the refrigerator and pulled open its stained door. Three packages sat on the top shelf wrapped in green garbage bags. He removed one and tossed it to me. I reached out to catch it. It was heavy and almost round.

Wayne said, "For a guy who likes mementoes, you're going to love this one."

I looked up at Wayne and, to my dismay, I saw he was holding a pistol that he'd hid in the refrigerator.

He smiled coldly at me and said, "Open it and see what I collect."

I pulled the frozen plastic bag open and peered into it. A woman's dead eyes met mine. Her hair was clumped with frost and blood. I shuddered in horror.

Chuckling, Wayne said, "Show it to your friend." I let Lilly peek into the bag and she gasped in disbelief.

Laughter came from Wayne, and he asked, "Do you like her? I hope you will, because the two of you will be sitting next to her very soon. They were whores just like your old Grand Ma or whoever it was you were whining about."

He looked at me, then at Lilly and with a big smile said, "Aren't you glad you visited?"

Tauntingly, he said, "You interrupted my evening just when I was going to go out and tie one on. Now it looks like I'll really have something to celebrate." He pulled a large meat cleaver from a rack next to a wooden chopping block and held it in his free hand.

"Hey, I need to show you around a bit more. Just leave my old girlfriend there on the kitchen table and let me show you my bathroom. I must say you two are well mannered. I wish more of my visitors could be as accommodating."

We walked down a hall to a small bathroom with Wayne poking his pistol into my back. The bathroom door was open, and we stepped in. He stood in the doorway and gestured to the bathtub.

"If you two would step into the bathtub, I'd appreciate it immensely. Isn't that odd how things work out? I just had this urge to clean the floor this afternoon and never had any inkling I'd have guests. Now the two of you're here and, I know it's rude, but I don't want to mess that floor up with globs of bloody gore as I slice and dice you. Enough talk; now let's get those wet clothes off."

Lilly spoke up and said, "Can we at least say a prayer?"

"Sure, while you take your clothes off. Just throw them onto the floor."

Lilly started chanting some of her strange prayers and

grasped the locket hanging around her neck.

Wayne said, "You ever hear of silent prayers? That mumbo jumbo shit drives me crazy." He was waving his gun around and irritation distorted his face.

Lilly prayed even harder, and suddenly she squeezed the locket hard and ripped it from her neck.

Just as she did, Wayne screamed out in pain, and the cleaver fell from his hand, impaling itself in his left foot. He grabbed for his stomach and started to crumple to the floor, the gun falling out of his hand. He cried out in anguish, and Lilly's voice grew even louder as she swung the locket around and around. Wayne wavered back and forth and suddenly vomited all over the floor. I jumped from the bathtub and dove for the puke-coated gun. Wayne had fallen on his face and continued screaming in terrible pain. Lilly continued to whirl the locket around and around as she chanted strange words I couldn't recognize.

Once we were both out of the bathtub and I had the vomit coated pistol in my hand, Lilly stopped her chanting and held the locket still.

Wayne still moaned, not even noticing Lilly stooping over to yank the cleaver from his foot. A trickle of blood flowed from his shoe when it was free of the cleaver.

She told him to stand up and take his clothes off.

He protested and said, "I can't stand. My head is spinning and my foot hurts so badly."

His protestation didn't work, and a few minutes later Lilly and I led him out to a place under the Banyan tree. He stood there naked, pleading for mercy.

Lilly told him to stay right where he was and not to move.

Blood flowed from his foot and puddled on the ground, mixing with the rain. He swayed back and forth, and above him the tree shook and swung its great branches to and fro.

Over the thunder and the noises coming from the frenzied Banyan tree, I could hear him sobbing. Another flash of lightning illuminated his body just as an aerial root shot down from the canopy and impaled him. The root punched through his shoulder and exited his stomach all the while tossing him about like a fish on a hook. He yelled in agony as tendrils from the root ripped him open and splayed open his chest letting his entrails cascade out over his legs. His cries of agony faded as his body was lifted deep into the canopy.

Lilly and I stood there watching in fascination as the tree seemed to celebrate its kill. Its gyrations went on for a long time, but after the rain stopped, its frenzied movements slowly abated.

Six months later I bought the old house at a sheriff's sale for just a fraction of its unpaid taxes. No one else wanted it since it was the home of a serial killer whose whereabouts were still unknown.

I still visit Lilly at her house of magic and promise her that, when I have a child, I want her to be its God Mother. How many kids have a Santeria priestess as a God Mother?

ONE EIGHTY SEVEN

The door flew open and a man flushed with anger waved a fist and yelled, "I'm going to kick your fucking fat ass, you God damn cock sucker. You sold me worthless insurance."

"Wait a minute," Mr. Taros said quietly to the giant of a man peering down at him from the other side of his desk. The big man was so angry that a vein on his forehead undulated beneath his skin like some alien life form. "Give me back my money or I'll shove your ugly head right up your ass," he yelled as his nostrils flared wide like those of a charging bull.

Mr. Taros slowly stood as he pushed back his chair, "I'll assure you, Mr. Callahan, if there's any problem with your insurance, you'll get every penny of your money back. Why don't you just sit down and let me get your files so we can take care of this issue immediately. Sir, would you like a cold soda?"

Callahan licked his lips and stood there glaring at Taros, then with a snort said, "Yeah, get me a Coke and get your fucking files and your checkbook. I want my money back."

Taros turned and replied, "Ice cold Coke coming up, sir." He turned away from Callahan and headed for the door labeled with a big sign reading 'storage.' The door was located directly behind Taros' desk. He quickly stepped through its threshold into a darkened room. He picked up his bulging briefcase, paused for a second, smiled broadly, and shouted back to Callahan, "Sorry to make you wait." Then he quietly exited out the back door. As he climbed down the back stairs he felt sorry that his bogus insurance business was already over, but he was still a couple million dollars richer and nobody had even got hurt. He smiled as he hailed a cab and sped away to his house just outside of Las Vegas. It was now time for a career change.

A week later, Mr. Taros became Chef Taros and found a position in one of the nicest casinos on the strip. His credentials might have been a bit fraudulent, but he could cook. In fact, he was an excellent cook, and the job offered him a way to work and stay out of the public's view for a while. It was like hiding in plain sight, right in the middle of Sin City.

Taros had a wife, Megan, and they had been together for many years. Most labeled them as an odd couple, and their assessment grew from numerous quirks the two demonstrated, but primarily it resulted from how they looked together. Megan looked like a Vegas showgirl with her surgically exaggerated features, and bubbly disposition, while Mr. Taros was squat with a visible paunch, bald as humpty dumpty, and displayed a very disagreeable demeanor. Regardless of what a toad he was, Megan loved him; the truth was that she loved him because he was a low life genius who would do anything to keep her happy; anything! He loved her and, oddly enough, she felt the same for him. He was her toad in shining armor, her confidante and her bad boy lover.

Taros' first name was John, but he hated it, so everyone called him Taros or Mr. Taros except, of course, for Megan. She called him John, and from her it sounded like music. Taros took care of Megan in style. His genius and dark sleazy side was always working to make Megan's life fun and carefree.

Taros provided money, a nice home, fashionable clothes and, of course, a plethora of food and drink.

John never had any formal education, but he was autodidactic and absorbed everything, including life's lessons, like a sponge. In addition, John possessed one other weird innate sense that sort of let him know how to do things that he'd never done before.

On top of everything else, they both soaked up all the street smarts available on the billion dollar avenues of Sin City. They could probably live nicely just from the smart street schooling available there. Bottom line, they just loved Vegas. John even liked how dry and warm it was.

Megan didn't have to work, but she liked to do interesting things, and one adventure she loved was working for a nine hundred sex line business.

She was thrilled at her spicy job, and she made a lot of money just juicing up the callers. She had all kinds of men and even women calling her. When she went home she'd share her phone adventures with John and tell him how difficult it was not to laugh as she played imaginary sex partners like Daddy's little girl, a naughty secretary, a sex starved nun, a Muslim woman masturbating under her burqa, or an Amazonian warrior commanding her sex slave to do all kinds of dirty little things. The one nine hundred sex talk adventure was a pretty neat job, because it heated up her sex life with John. However, a few months into the job, the owner, some guy from Iran, just disappeared. Without him, the place closed up and Megan was back home, bored.

Soon after her sex talk gig, Megan got another fun pastime as a paramedic. It didn't pay worth a shit, but she didn't care because it was just so much fun to zoom around to accidents, see the gore, and pick up dead people. Anyway, with John's job as a chef, it let them have a lot of extra money that she used for putting gourmet food on their table.

Just when Megan was really getting good at her fun new job, they fired her over some irregularities with her paperwork. An internal audit of her books showed discrepancies of charging for more deliveries to the hospitals and morgues than they claimed they received.

As luck would have it, John also lost his job shortly thereafter. The casino claimed that John's signature dishes weren't prepared with the same perfection as before and subsequently lacked the taste they were famous for. Specifically, the meat from his new vendor lacked the tenderness and freshness of what he'd previously been buying. John asked for more time to find a new source, but they wouldn't give it to him, and on payday he was fired.

It didn't make much difference to John and Megan Taros because they both had decided to start their own business.

The new venture was called the Eat Rite Weight Loss Program. The company was small; in fact, it just consisted of Megan sitting in her splendid living room talking to her 1-900-eat-rite callers and John making the eat rite pills right there in their kitchen.

They did an ad on TV targeting all the areas of the USA where the fattest people lived and started getting hundreds of orders. It was amazing; they had stacks of money pouring in. The pills were a little addictive because John had added cannabis oil along with some cocaine to them.

Their ad claimed you didn't even have to change your eating habit or exercise at all.

People love it when you tell them "don't change a thing, just pop our pills and you'll soon look and feel like a million dollars." People were buying their pills like, well like psychedelic drugs of the sixties.

Anyway, the money was coming in so fast that John got a bit nervous and decided to rethink his business plan and reinvent themselves. Reinventing was something they were good at.

The new plan meant charging a lot more per client, and that meant they had to convince new patients that they really needed their treatment. They decided the target market would be the critically ill, severely obese patients who were probably not much longer for planet earth. Now they needed a human guinea pig or two to test their concoction. They altered a few pictures of a 1400 pound guy, changing his face and the picture's background. It became part of their award winning ad showing the results of six months of using their amazing Brazilian fat-be-gone treatment. The ad said, "The

Brazilian magical drug should only be used by those suffering from acute obesity. If your fat is squishing out your life,
you need Dr. Brazil's Fat-be-gone pills. Please call our
1-900-fat-gone hot line for a consultation with one of our
compassionate, loving weight loss professionals."

The ad was again an overwhelming success. Fat people
from Louisiana, Oklahoma, Texas, Alabama, Nevada, and
God knows where were calling and whining about their
weight problems. They told Megan of their overeating disor-
ders, hormone imbalances, and a plethora of other reasons
why they weighed a quarter of a ton or more. Megan and
John both worked the lines and got all the poop about each
applicant. They were looking for some pretty sick ones;
some who wouldn't be around much longer without their
professional intervention. They had three candidates who
were really promising, then bingo, they got just the right
guy. He was about 860 pounds give or take twenty.

His name was Raymond Billings. Raymond was just
23 years old and, as luck would have it, lived just on the out-
skirts of Las Vegas. He'd been stuck in a room in his mom's
house for the last five years. I mean really stuck. He'd grown
wider than the door or its two windows. Raymond was the
room's prisoner.

During the phone interview, Megan had asked Raymond
all kinds of questions to make sure he was the right person
for their trial run of their treatment. His sad confession
sealed the decision of who they would first assist.

She asked Raymond if he'd ever had anything to do with
women before he got so obese and he told her his sad tale.

When he was only seventeen and could still just barely

get around, he'd met some lady of the night who said she'd do it with him for thirteen dollars, which was all the cash Raymond had with him. She got into his vehicle and they drove off into the desert to do it. When they finally parked and Raymond looked at the hooker, he could tell she'd soured a bit about the whole deal. She told him she hadn't noticed how big he was until she got in, and now all he could get for thirteen dollars was maybe a hand job and she'd show him her large breasts.

Well, no girl had never ever even touched his magic wand, so to Raymond it actually sounded okay. It was absolutely a step in the right direction. What was that saying, that a bird in her hand was worth two in her bush or how did it go?

So he unzipped his fly, poked around a bit and discovered there was no way he could free the bird unless he just slid down his pants. When he did, his lady friend's eyes bulged open in obvious dismay, but she went ahead and tried to fulfill her end of the deal. She reached over and started searching for his magic wand. After some sweaty and frustrating moments she thought she found the illusive little guy. She wiggled and tugged on it to make sure it was what she was looking for, then suddenly it exploded. She jumped back just in time to see the steering wheel and console plastered with dangling strands of something that looked like overcooked rice noodles. That was Raymond's first introduction to sex with a woman.

Now years later, he still had that urge that the one thing he wanted to do most was to have sex with a real woman before he died. Megan, being a real sweetie, felt Raymond's plight and vowed that she and John would help Raymond before he went off into the hereafter. He was the perfect candidate for the trial run of their new diet magic pills.

Raymond's story was pitiful. He'd never really got to enjoy life. It was sad, because here he was living in Sin City and had been denied about every enjoyable sin one could name; well, maybe not totally sin free. He was certainly guilty of lust, big time on gluttony, and the same went for greed. Then there was, of course, his filthy habits of throwing things onto the floor, soiling his PJ's, not cleaning himself, soaking the couch in urine, belching, and constant flatulating. Now, granted that was a side effect of his sin of gluttony, but it's like man's law; if one crime causes another crime, you got to do the time. Raymond sure as hell knew that eating three whole chickens, two quarts of potato salad, and a quart of baked beans was going to give him some natural gas problems.

Then there's the issue that Raymond would often get angry and throw things around his bedroom. You're going to say it's because the poor man was frustrated from living his life as a prisoner in a single room, but regardless of the reason it was wrath, and wrath was sin. Only one individual can get away with throwing a temper tantrum and that's the big kahuna sitting up there in the sky on His golden throne.

What about Raymond's envy problem? It seemed like every time Raymond saw a girl kiss a guy he'd seethe with envy; and what about that time the gardener dropped in to show Raymond his little collection of steamy karma sutra poses with two hot babes who were as naked as the day they were born. He got so jealous that he yelled, screamed, and cried for fifteen minutes after he saw those pictures. That was jealousy and a major fit of wrath.

Raymond was certainly not sin-free. Raymond had committed six of the seven deadly sins without even lifting his ass off the steel reinforced couch he sat on for the last five years.

You'd have to ask yourself, if poor Raymond was to escape the confines of that room, what sins would he then commit? Perhaps with help from Megan and her genius husband, Raymond might just get the chance.

John looked over his application and finally stamped his approval to the document. Megan and John loved Raymond, and they were going to help him. Raymond was now approved for the extended fat reduction treatment and was sent his first six months of pills. Raymond had agreed to the Eat Rite Weight Loss program's terms to pay $999 a month for each month he lost fifty pounds or more.

Raymond had to take the pills as the instructions directed and promise that six months after he reached his optimal weight for his height he'd honor Mr. and Mrs. Taros with a visit to their home as their dinner guest.

If Raymond broke any terms of their agreement, the contract would be null and void. Megan warned Raymond that most likely he'd also quickly return to his former weight.

Raymond started the pills and noticed immediately a change in his mood and desire to live. It wasn't enough motivation to stop him from eating all day long, but he knew something was different.

Raymond's visiting physician, Dr. Hardwood, was first to notice what was different. He was elated to discover that his critically obese patient had somehow lost fifty pounds. Raymond still seemed to be eating as much as ever, but miraculously his fat seemed to be melting away.

Dr. Hardwood did a whole battery of blood tests. When he got the results back he was shocked yet pleasantly surprised that they all came back positive.

On Raymond's second month of secretly taking the Fat-be-gone pills he lost another seventy pounds. He loved this new pill. He could eat all he wanted and still lose weight. Raymond was like a living food processor; he could eat an entire roasted chicken, and in less than an hour he was popping its remains out as chicken nuggets. It seemed things just flowed right through him so fast that they didn't have time to be digested. His body was instead eating away its own fat. He was always hungry.

Dr. Hardwood was shocked to find that Raymond had shed another seventy pounds on the second month. This time he called Unger Pharmaceutical, the manufacturer of the diet pill he'd prescribed to Raymond three months prior. He told the company rep that Raymond was the perfect poster child for their unbelievable diet pill. He told the rep all about Raymond losing 120 pounds in only two months and that he still ate like a horse. He told them how Raymond's blood work all came back perfect, and even his heart rate and blood pressure were significantly improved.

The third month Raymond lost 115 pounds, and now an army of dieticians and specialists were at his beckon call. Everyone wanted to claim some of the glory for shrinking hundreds of pounds of fat off Raymond. His prognosis had changed from checking out soon to a guy who was as healthy as a horse. While the pounds dropped off, his skin just seemed to shrink right back into place. Better yet, sometimes when he awoke from his frequent naps he thought he was getting some strange sensations down in his nether region. There was no way he could reach it or see it, so he just daydreamed about what he'd be like in a few more months.

On the end of the sixth month he was down to 187 pounds and Dr. Hardwood told him that was his optimal, the absolutely perfect weight for his height and physique.

Raymond was looking really buff and he no longer smelled like rotting blue cheese. The old steel-reinforced couch with its big round poopy hole had been tossed out. Raymond was now forced to learn to take control of his bodily functions and felt elated that he didn't have to sit over the top of what his mom called the poopy potty, a big 24 inch diameter galvanized tub.

Now he could take care of himself.

Raymond even had a job as an Unger Pharmaceutical's poster boy. The job earned him a lot of money, and girls and even some guys were lustfully looking and smiling at him. In fact, he'd gained so much fame shedding all those pounds that he now had an agent to handle his business dealings.

The Unger Pharmaceuticals' lead poster boy job simply consisted of looking good and having a lot of hot chicks around him. At first he acted like Jethro Bodine of "The Beverly Hillbillies," but then he started getting more suave. They taught him etiquette and how to dress and how to answer questions and even how to sit while being interviewed. He excelled at his new calling and quickly transformed himself into the new Raymond Billings. He tried to forget the ugly life he'd just escaped. He didn't want to remember piss-

ing through a catheter for years or the embarrassing moments where he'd be talking to someone and a trickle of
urine would splatter into the big tub beneath his ass.
He didn't want anyone to know these things. They were all
just a terrible embarrassment to him. His goal now was to
enjoy life that had been denied him for the last five years.

He dove big-time into his new persona. His publicist recognized the fact that he seemed to just stay at this magical
weight of one hundred and eighty-seven pounds. He told
Raymond that they needed to play that up. They would do
pieces that always talked about the one hundred and eighty-
seven. He'd seed an audience with women who would
scream, "One eighty seven." Soon thousands of women
would be screaming "One eighty seven, one eighty seven."
That would be what people would remember him for and, of
course, his handsome good looks.

A month after he'd reinvented himself as simply Raymond, he met a model who seduced him.

She was visiting Vegas for the "Adult Video Awards." Her
screen name was Bambi Richards and she was the current
winner of the Best Oral Sex Scene and Best Anal Sex Scene
by a solo actress. She'd also won the same awards the previous year. After the show, they went out to dinner together to
celebrate her victories.

Bambi became very forward as she sensed she had a virgin
in her presence. She'd never been with a virgin of either sex,
and the fact that this was the famous Raymond whose picture was plastered all over billboards and TV screens en-
thralled her.

Bambi coyly asked Raymond, "Would you come up to my

room at the Luxor and work with me on some scenes from my upcoming movie? I need someone to practice with, and I hate the guys I work with. And you're so handsome." She giggled like a school girl.

Raymond was thrilled, but petrified for this chance to finally have sex with a woman. He managed to utter, "Sure, I'd love to help you. When did you want to practice?"

Bambi cooed, "Can we start tonight or is that too soon?"

Raymond felt so much fear that he thought he'd piss himself from the weird sensations that went through him thinking about the fact he was finally at twenty four going to be in bed with a real woman; not just any woman either, but the AVN award winner for two years in a row for "Best Oral Sex and Anal Sex." He looked at the two big awards sitting on their table with Bambi Richards inscribed into their glistening surfaces and said, "Sure, Bambi, let's do it tonight.

After he said it, he realized it sounded a little vulgar, but she was asking him to come to her room and have sex so why should he worry about being crass.

An hour later after multiple drinks and a few puffs on a joint, Bambi had commandeered from their taxi driver, she was waiting spread eagled for him on her giant bed.

Bambi motioned to him with pursed lips and said, "Come on, Raymond. I'm not going to bite you. You got to help me. Come over here and kiss me."

Raymond crawled across the bed in a drugged and drunken stupor, pressed his lips against Bambi's, and felt her tongue push in and out of his mouth. Suddenly, he didn't even care what kind of fool he was going to make of himself; he just wanted to do it. He awkwardly crawled onto her and found to his dismay that he'd exploded again almost instantly, but this time it didn't expire. It was still as rigid as it was before he did it. The fog in his head from the joint faded, and in its place was animal lust as he discovered that not only had he lost all that weight, but he'd gained total control of his penis. It seemed to have its own life, and it wanted to be with Bambi.

The next morning after getting only a little over an hour of sleep, he found Bambi staring down at him as he blinked his eyes open.

She said, "Raymond, you were wonderful. You made me feel so good last night. If you want a career in adult videos, I promise you, you'd be a star. You're incredible. You're sexier than two men at once and, believe me, I should know." She giggled and continued, "The ladies would just love you."

Later that afternoon as Raymond was digesting all that had happened to him during the last few days, he realized what a miracle life he had. He'd gained a lot of self esteem just by shedding all those 600 pounds. He also was proud that Dr. Hardwood and the people from Unger Pharmaceuticals wanted him as their poster boy. He was making a shit load of money, and then last night. Wow! Life was good!

Most of all, he was happy that he was now so handsome that women just flocked to him and that he knew what to do with his groveling horde of followers. His agent was calling him a cooter magnet. He didn't like it; it sounded demeaning to women, but he did like what it meant.

By the end of January Raymond had become engaged to seven different beautiful models. At least that was what leaked out from the gossip rags. According to the news stories and a few lawsuits, each woman had been sworn to secrecy by Raymond, and he'd promised each of them that he'd announce the engagement on the "Jay Leno Show" a week before Valentine's Day.

The day arrived that Raymond promised he'd tell the whole world who the lucky woman would be. Most of the audience felt they already knew because Raymond had brought a hot porno star with him as his companion to the show. She was sitting in the audience with a smile stretched across her beaming face. When Raymond marched out onto the stage as Jay Leno's guest, the crowd roared with enthusiasm. Once they settled down, Jay turned to Raymond and asked him, "So Raymond, are you going to tell the nation who's the lucky lady?"

Raymond looked baffled and said, "Are you talking about my date in the audience?" The cameras focused on Pamela Puma. She waved and threw kisses at Raymond sitting next to Jay Leno.

Jay replied, "Is she one of the secret seven who are waiting for you to disclose which one will be the future Mrs. Raymond Billings?"

Raymond replied with a grin, "No, Ms. Puma isn't one of them because there aren't any women that I'm engaged to or have been. This story is just a vicious rumor perpetuated by some gossip rag hag who concocted the tale to help sell more copies of their papers. It's no different than the stories of Ms. Big Foot hiding in a cave in West Virginia with her lover Elvis Presley.

"There probably are seven demented women who somehow mistook my kindness to them as something more."

Jay Leno said, "Well, there you have it. The most wanted bachelor is still available to some lucky lady."

While Leno was talking, a devastated Pamela Puma left the studio. On the news that evening it was reported that one of Raymond's jilted ladies was found dead in her bathtub. The report stated that the distraught former fiancé of celebrity superstar Raymond Billings had apparently slit her wrist and bled to death. A note on her bed indicated that she'd been very hurt by Raymond's national TV rejection of her. Ms. Puma wrote that she couldn't live without Raymond, and she couldn't stand the humiliation he'd heaped on her by denying their engagement ever existed.

Two days later another of the seven women who claimed to have received a marriage proposal from Raymond drove her smart car at nearly a hundred miles per hour into a parked bulldozer, instantly killing herself. She left behind a similar suicide note.

There was a media firestorm as thousands of journalists tried to figure out if the seven women claiming he'd proposed to them were all just plain insane or was Raymond the heartless philistine philanderer they claimed he was. The two women who had committed suicide over his rejection had identical Cubic Zirconia engagement rings in their possession at the time of their death. An undercover investigator claimed a clerk from the famed "Zirconia Forever Store" in Las Vegas recalled selling twenty-five of the fifty dollar imitation diamond rings to Raymond Billings.

To complicate things worse, three of the jilted seven were now claiming publically that they were carrying Raymond's love child.

While all this was going on, Raymond was partying at the famed Rooster Ranch just outside of Vegas. He'd challenged his new acquaintance, football superstar Hotdog Williams, to a match of endurance. The two had holed up at the bordello for most of the day in a neck and neck battle of who can out-screw the other. Raymond was ahead by two prostitutes, but Hotdog Williams wasn't tiring and seemed to be savoring each conquest more than Raymond. When Raymond stopped to grab something to eat, Williams pulled ahead of him by three. Sixteen hours later Williams was ahead by seven, and Raymond was so tired and weak he fell asleep on top of his last conquest. When she pushed him off, he made a couple murmurs, but fell right back to sleep.

When Hotdog Williams heard his challenger had fallen asleep, he had Dolly Angel, the bordello's Madame, tally up the official score and post it on their scoreboard of "Major League Fuckers." The score was:

Hotdog Williams 28   *Raymond Billings 16*

When Raymond finally woke up and went down to the bordello's living room, the ladies started giggling, cheering and asking if there was going to be a rematch. Raymond looked a bit dazed at first, then he looked at the Tally Board and saw he'd loss by twelve. He was embarrassed. In fact, he felt so humiliated that Williams had outlasted him and fucked twelve more hookers than he had; it made him feel like a real loser. Making it even more humiliating, was the fact he was also stuck with a fucking bill of almost eight thousand dollars.

Raymond tried to smile at the ladies, but inside he was

steaming angry. Williams must have cheated was all he could think. They must have padded the numbers just to make him look bad. He hated that smug bastard. He didn't even have the decency to wait for him before he left. Now Raymond would have to call a cab. Some of the ladies tried to cheer him up and said it wasn't the quantity, it was the quality, and you're a much better lover than old Hotdog. It didn't make him feel any better.

When the cab came, he was sure the driver would say something like, "So old Hotdog Williams is a better fucker than you?" or "Heard you fell asleep on the job. Yuck yuck!" The news wasn't out yet, but it would be, he was sure.

During a Valentine's morning interview with Ross Truax of "Good Morning USA," Raymond responded to some of the accusations by the jilted models. Raymond looked at Ross and said, "You know Ross, when a celebrity gives a little attention to some unknown, the media is going to make something big of it. When a woman is the recipient of the attention, the whole world instantly makes it into some sort of romance. Incidentally, Ross, did you hear about the discovery in China of a warehouse that held over a hundred thousand counterfeit copies of my latest 187 calendar; the one with me wearing a loin cloth?"

Ross asked, "Is that also the one of you wearing nothing, but the gigantic horn of a Watusi bull between your legs?"

Raymond chuckled, "Yes, Ross that's the one. Girls love that picture. I probably have autographed a few thousand copies of it."

"That horn looked heavy. How did you hold that thing in

place without it falling off?"

"Ross, you sly fox. You know how I hold it on; I just fill it up with me and think about some hot model and nature does the rest."

The audience broke into laughter as a large picture lowered from the ceiling of Raymond wearing nothing but the Watusi bull horn.

As the laughter subsided, Ross asked, "Isn't that lady kneeling next to you hugging your legs one of the models who claimed she was engaged to you?

Raymond studied the picture for a long moment and said, "Ross, you're absolutely correct. She's one of those women. I can't remember her name, but she's one of them."

Ross said, "Her name was Monica. Monica Mercedes and she said you told her you loved her and wanted to marry her. Is she lying?"

Raymond laughed a little and shook his head in disbelief, "Ross, well to tell you the truth I say that to a lot of my fans. Women like to feel they're beautiful and appreciated, but it's just a compliment. You know like, 'Wow you're beautiful, I'd love to marry you or I look at some beautiful woman and say, 'You're so beautiful, I love you.' It's harmless compliments. Women want to hear those words. It makes them feel good."

Raymond gestured to the audience and asked, "Don't you love to hear those words I love you?"

The audience erupted in, "Yes, Raymond, we love you, too." Others yelled, "Raymond, you're so hotttttt!"

"Really, Ross, we celebrities always have bad things said about us regardless of how nice we try to be. I tried to make seven women happy and this is what I get. I'm a heartbreaker, a dream killer, an insensitive philistine philanderer. Does anyone ever consider how I must feel being constantly attacked like that? Well, I think my attackers are mostly a lot of very sick people, jealous of all my accomplishments. I really don't want to talk about them any longer."

At the end of the interview, Ross asked, "Well, Raymond, now comes the big question. Are you still eating whatever you want and miraculously maintaining your optimal weight? Are you still that one eighty seven?"

Raymond smiled and said, "I think you want more than my word."

When he said that, stage hands brought out a very impressive scale. Raymond looked at the scales in mock inquisitiveness and asked, "Is that for - me?"

The audience echoed back, "Yes!" Others started chanting, "One eighty seven, one eighty seven."

Raymond waved his hand to the audience for silence as he strolled across the stage to the awaiting scales. He stood there pretending to dread stepping onto the scales. Some women in the audience started chanting, "Do it, do it, Raymond." Others were yelling, "Raymond, you're so hot. Yeah, do it!"

All of a sudden, Raymond started gyrating his hips as he did an impromptu striptease down to his boxer shorts. The audience roared again, and some ladies yelled, "Take it all off, Raymond."

After what seemed like an eternity, a smiling Raymond stepped proudly onto the scales, nonchalantly drinking a sixteen ounce bottle of Coke. Confidence and pride exuded from him. He let out a huge burp and suddenly the audience broke out in bedlam again shouting in a thunderous roar, "One eighty seven, one eighty seven, one eighty seven." After thirty seconds of the roar, the show's host quieted the ecstatic crowd.

The host said, "Well, to make sure we have a person here who's bright enough to read a scale, I invited Terry Blackstone, president of the New York State Weights & Measures Association." With that introduction, Blackstone strolled upon the stage and waved to the crowd. A weak applause rippled through the crowd along with a few shouts of, "Weigh, Raymond; weigh, Raymond."

Blackstone started to walk over to Ross, but Ross motioned him over to Raymond, still standing proudly on the scale waving at his excited fans and throwing kisses to admiring ladies.

When Blackstone stood next to Raymond, Ross asked, "Mr. Blackstone, do you know how much those boxer shorts weigh that Raymond is wearing?"

"Coincidently, Ross, I do. In fact, in my pocket I have a pair of boxer shorts that are identical to what Raymond is now wearing."

Ross added, "I think if anyone studied the boxer shorts that Mr. Blackstone has, they would find Raymond's DNA on them because, ladies these shorts were worn by Raymond right before the show."

Another huge uproar went through the crowd.

Raymond motioned to Blackstone to hand him the shorts. He said jokingly, "I can't even leave my shorts around anymore before someone tries to steal them. Mr. Blackstone, do you really want these?" before he could reply Raymond added, "I wonder if his wife knows?" With that he flung the shorts out into the audience. A stampede of women dove for the descending shorts. Women elbowed, bit and shoved each other to catch the slightly used shorts. Finally a large woman waved them triumphantly above her head as she giggled hysterically.

Once the audience was calmed down, Ross asked, "Mr. Blackstone, did you adjust the scale to take into account the weight of Raymond's undershorts?"

"Oh yes, Ross, we certainly did. We have checked the scales and they're adjusted perfectly."

A big drum roll started as Ross said, "Okay Mr. Blackstone, do your stuff and tell us how much Raymond weighs. Please read the numbers out loud."

Mr. Blackstone said, "Okay! The weight is One hundred. He paused for effect and then put his head down closer to the scales and said "One hundred and ninety six."

Raymond looked smug standing on the scale as the audience applauded and then the announced numbers started to register and the audience yelling quickly died away. There were confused looks on many faces. Someone yelled, "Hey Blackstone you need glasses!" But mostly silence prevailed.

Raymond recovered from the shock, said, "Mr. Weight expert, I think you better look again, because I'm one eighty seven."

Ross, the host walked over to the scale and glanced down at the read out and shook his head saying, "Well something is wrong Raymond because they do read one hundred ninety six. Why don't you step off of it and we will have it adjusted."

Mr. Blackstone took a two pound stainless steel test weight from a drawer under the scale and placed it on the scales. He looked at the readout and it displayed exactly two pounds. The audience was totally silent. Something unbelievable had happened. Raymond was no longer his optimal weight. He was now one hundred and ninety six.

Ross apologized to Raymond, "I'm sorry Raymond, sometimes things don't go the way we planned them. You look a bit peaked, why don't we have you back once you see what's wrong. We all still love you even if you're a couple of pounds heavier."

Raymond recovered enough to say, "Thank you Ross and I'll be back." He waved at the audience and walked off of the stage.

Something was wrong. In fact something was very wrong this morning when he woke up. He had a beautiful blond nymphet named Collette over for the night and they had frolicked for hours. In the morning Raymond awoke to Collette trying to give him a little morning treat, but unbelievably he was as flaccid as a string of over cooked spaghetti. Now that was something he'd never experienced before. He told himself that Collette was just not that sexy. It was her fault. Sober and in the sunlight she didn't look as young as he'd remembered and my God those big hooters, nineteen inch waist and rotund butt just made her look so fake.

He'd pushed it out of his mind as he prepared for the early morning show. He'd decided he just couldn't sleep with old ugly women or these things would continue to happen. He rushed to the studio and Collette was forgotten. But now his failures started to really scare him. He remembered his promise to the Fat-be-Gone people and sort of forgotten as the fat fell away. He wondered if his promise had really meant something to them? The main thing was that he needed to get more of those stupid "Dr. Brazil's Fat-be-Gone" pills. He was convinced that his problems would be solved by those wonderful pills.

When he got back to his flat, he hunted around for their phone number. In fact, he tore his apartment apart, but the phone number wasn't anywhere to be found.

He was beginning to panic when he thought maybe they still had ads on TV.

He flipped around on the TV for over an hour and finally gave up and sat there on the couch in his underwear, crying. He'd fucked up. He'd broken his promise. His eyes filled with tears as he thought about what he knew was going to come. He didn't want to be fat again. God, no. He asked himself why he'd been such an ass, and more tears started to fall. He pictured himself sitting on that heavy plastic-covered couch with the shit hole cut right into the middle of it. Christ, why did he fuck up? Why?

He wiped away more tears, smashed his hand down on his leg, and saw that his skin wasn't smooth any longer. He had stretch marks; big stretch marks. He reached with trepidation to his crotch and felt what he'd feared, his penis had also shrunk down to almost nothing. This was an emergency. He needed those pills again. He needed his treatment. He wouldn't be able to see anyone in this condition. He'd lose everything. Suddenly from the TV, he heard the ad, "Are you obese and need etc"

He glanced over to the TV just as a phone number slowly

scrolled across the screen. It was the magic number. A great sigh of relief ushered from his lungs as he started to parrot the number over and over while he frantically searched for his phone. He couldn't find it. This was one hell of a day for Raymond and he started cursing, "God, where did I leave it? What the fuck did I do with my phone?" Suddenly, he remembered, it was in his suit jacket pocket.

Retrieving it, he noticed all the calls he'd missed. It had been set on vibrate when he was on the show and he never turned the sound back on. Right now he didn't give a shit about all the calls. He didn't care if the President or the Pope called; he needed his pills, his treatment.

He dialed the number that he'd been reciting over and over in his head and waited for someone to answer the call. He paced the floor and silently cursed under his breath. "Please answer," he kept muttering.

Finally someone answered the call and started a sales pitch, but he quickly interrupted and said he was supposed to visit the company's owner on Valentine's Day. He asked if he could talk to the boss.

The woman said, "Please wait."

He waited for what seemed like an eternity and finally a woman came back and said, "May I help you?" It sounded like the same person who had initially answered the phone, but he didn't care; he just wanted his pills. "Yes, I was supposed to visit your company's owners on Valentine's Day, and I sort of forgot. I was calling to see where I'm to go or if I'm too late."

The voice on the other end said, "Oh, this must be Raymond. Of course you're not too late. This is still Valentine's

Day. We'd love you to come over maybe for dinner. Would that be good for you?"

"Yes, I'd love to. By the way do you have anymore of your diet pills? Maybe I could pick them up at dinner tonight? I think I need some more."

She hesitated for a moment or two, then said, "Raymond, don't you fear. You come on over and we're going to fix you all up. I've seen you on TV and we're so proud of what you've been able to accomplish. I'm going to have one of my assistants give you directions to our home. My husband and I'll be so looking forward to meeting you in the flesh. Oh before I forget, please bring one of those calendars with you that you talked about on the show this morning. All my friends want them. Bye, sweetie!"

The line was dead for a moment or two, then another lady introduced herself who oddly again sounded just like the owner. She gave Raymond the directions and he decided to go over to their home right away. He couldn't believe how close they lived.

In less than an hour Raymond had dressed, called a cab, and was speeding across Vegas to their home. When he arrived, Megan watched him from her kitchen window. She saw Raymond pay the cab driver, who had also noticed the 187 calendars. Apparently he asked Raymond for one and Raymond smilingly obliged. To Raymond's total amazement, the cabbie got back into his cab and didn't ask for an autograph. In fact, the cabbie didn't even notice that the person he was hauling around Vegas was the century's most sought after bachelor. The shock and hurt in Raymond's face was clearly visible. Things weren't going well for him at all. In fact, when Raymond stooped over to pull a calendar out of the pile on the back seat, he noticed his stomach hung out over his belt and two of his shirt buttons had popped loose when he straightened back up. A bulge of stomach protruded through the hole where the buttons had been. He stood for a moment, then positioned the bundle of 187 calendars to cover the bulge of his protruding stomach. As he walked up the sidewalk, he looked like he was on the verge of a total mental breakdown.

When he reached the front door, he held back for a moment or two before he rang the door bell. Just as he gathered himself together and was reaching for the bell, Megan flung open the door. He was startled and totally flustered.

Megan had dressed in her usual sexy way for Valentine's Day and welcomed Raymond with a big smile. She said, "I'm so excited to have such a big celebrity in my own house for Valentine's dinner."

She wrapped her arms around him and gave him a big hug, pushing her large breasts into his chest. Raymond hesitantly hugged her back, feeling uneasy about being there, but he needed those fucking pills. He'd do anything for a prescription of six more months of them. He knew he had some major ass kissing to set things right. First he had to apologize for breaking his original promises to them. Of all the people to have broken a promise with, why did he do it to them?

Megan gushed, "Your call was such a big surprise; we'd just figured you'd totally forgotten us."

Raymond noticed that Megan was wearing a stained

apron over a very elegant red dress with hearts all over it. He'd also noticed that Megan's legs were shapely and ended in some very sexy four inch gloss red high heels.

"Come in, come in. There's no need for you to stand out there in the heat."

He stepped into the foyer and realized she was staring up at him and shaking her head, displaying a huge smile. She said, "I just can't believe it. I just can't believe we're finally meeting face to face. You're such a handsome young man and so sexy. Do you know Raymond, I have been out in the audience almost every time you did an interview or a show?" She held her arms out toward him with her wrists crossed and said, "I'm guilty of stalking, so I guess you need to arrest me and take me away with you." She giggled as she held her crossed wrists out to him.

Raymond didn't know what to say and just stared at her.

Suddenly she reached up to his face with both hands, tipped his face down to hers, and said, looking into his eyes, "Raymond, I'm just kidding. You look a little confused. Don't be. You're here for our celebration dinner. My husband and I want to get to know you better. We see you as our very own protégée."

Megan continued, "I have to say, Raymond, I'm so happy you remembered our invitation because my husband would have been so angry if you hadn't. He's been looking forward to this day for so long. He'll be so excited to see you. In fact, most of the day he's been fretting whether you'd come or not."

"Well, I'm looking forward to meeting him also," replied Raymond nervously. He'd lost his gift of gab and his previous confidence. A day prior, he would have tried to seduce

Megan or at least fondle her a bit. Those perky big breasts would have at least got one grope, but today he was too shy to even ask if could use their bathroom.

Megan said, "Please excuse my manners. I didn't mean to have you standing in the foyer all day while I talk your ears off."

Megan grabbed Raymond by his arm and pulled him into their dining room. It was an elegant room with a high ceiling and robin egg blue walls.

Megan pointed to a door on the opposite side of the room and told Raymond that it led to their kitchen. Behind it, Raymond could hear a man humming and the occasional clank of a pop or pan.

Megan motioned to Raymond to sit at her beautifully appointed dining table. In its middle, a beautiful candelabra sat with flickering candles. Beautiful china with little hearts was laid out on the table, accompanied by elegant silverware engraved with cupids on their handles.

Megan constantly looked him up and down said, "Raymond, let's drink a toast to a wonderful dinner and a beautiful Valentine's."

"Okay!" he said weakly. "When will your husband be joining us?"

"Well, my John, Mr. Taros, is busy putting together the Valentine's dinner, but I know he'll be so glad to see you. We were so worried you wouldn't show up. Do you know that my husband has worked in all the big Vegas casinos? Now he has his very own catering company. I'm so proud of him; he's just so busy. I mean, between our little pill business and the catering. He just works his buns off all the time."

"Let me go and tell him you're here. And you need to calm down! You need a drink. Here, let me pour you a nice big glass of wine. Now drink it down while I check on preparations for dinner."

Megan left Raymond sitting at the candlelit dining table. He looked around the room at the paneled walls covered with a multitude of pictures, and across from him was a framed poster of the Seven Deadly Sins. He glanced down the list and read the last one, Pride. He snorted as he remembered his mother saying to him, "Too much pride is a bad thing," and some saying like "pride goeth before the fall." Above the poster was a framed biblical proverb that read, "Proverb 18:7 A fool's mouth is his undoing, and his lips are a snare to his soul."

The room was cold. It was actually chilly, but he didn't care because the main thought occupying his mind was if and when he could get more of Dr. Brazil's Fat-be-Gone pills. He told himself he'd ask Megan for just one when she returned. He was sure she'd say yes, because she appeared to be nice and sincerely liked him even with his twenty pound or so weight gain. If he could just get one pill, it would make him feel so much better.

Megan came back into the dining room, all smiling and happy looking. She said, "Raymond, my husband is ready to show you around his kitchen. He's so proud of it. Come with me."

Just as she said that, Mr. Taros opened the kitchen door and introduced himself. "Hello, Raymond, I'm Mr. Taros. I'm so happy and honored you could make it. I was worrying about you earlier."

He stood there looking over at Raymond and added, "I want you to know you're really welcome to our home even if you did fudge a little on our deal." He winked at Raymond as he added, "You did live up to most of our contract, which is better than a lot of ungrateful people we help. Raymond, do you know a lot of the people we help never visit us after all we do for them. That hurts Megan. Well, come on, the longer we dally, the later dinner will be."

Megan added, "Yes, let's not waste any time. I want to have our wonderful Valentine's dinner sometime tonight. These things are so hard to plan."

She pulled Raymond to the kitchen door, and Mr. Taros moved aside to let them in.

Raymond looked at the huge kitchen. It wasn't just an ordinary kitchen; it was something that Taros had furnished with stainless steel tables, shelves, and racks. The kitchen had all kinds of equipment; big saws, meat slicers, you name it, it had it. Megan turned around to face Raymond and, glowing with excitement, said, "See what a beautiful kitchen we have? Isn't this unbelievable?"

Raymond nodded yes to Megan and said, "It certainly is a wonderful kitchen; a very professional looking one." Then he realized that he was walking on a kitchen floor covered with thick plastic sheeting. He hated sheets of plastic. So many years he'd lived with his couch encased in plastic and plastic sheets on his bedroom floor just to keep him from messing things up with his urine, shit, or whatever else he happened to expel from his 850 pound body. For a split second more Raymond wondered why the floor in this large beautiful kitchen was covered with plastic sheets, then it struck him.

Taros slammed his 32 ounce tenderizing mallet down on Raymond's head so hard you could hear teeth splintering. The blow toppled Raymond over onto an adjacent steel preparation table, his head making a dull metallic thud as it impacted the table's hard stainless steel surface. Raymond started to slide off, but his arm got caught on the meat slicer bolted to the table. Blood poured out over the table's surface from Raymond's cracked open skull.

Mr. Taros, in his excitement, proclaimed, "He's going to make a beautiful Valentine's dinner." A whoosh of air expelled from his lungs as he jumped into the air and swung the meat tenderizing mallet down on Raymond's skull once again. This time he cracked it open so far that part of Raymond's brain pushed out.

Megan moved over to her husband's side and gave him a big hug. She licked a little of the splattered blood from his face. John returned the gesture. His glittering beady eyes locked on Megan's adoring face and he lovingly exclaimed, "Damn you're so sexy."

She whispered sweetly in his ear as she reached around to touch his tail, "You're such a wonderful little devil."

Mr. Taros looked lustfully at his curvy wife as he broke open Raymond's skull to pull out his brains.

Holding the bloody grey mass in his hand, he said, "Fresh is the only way to eat them." He slapped the still warm organ down on the stainless steel table and said, "Sweetheart, I'm going to make one of your favorite snacks, a delicious sauté brain sandwich served on a sesame seed bun slathered with mustard and horseradish. And on the side a nice fat kosher pickle with a slice of red onion; just the way you like it."

Megan looked at her husband, slicing up Raymond's brain, and felt so blessed. He loved her that was obvious. She could tell because her husband's little knobby tail had pushed itself out of his beltline and was flipping about excitedly. Even more telling was the fact that his huge engorged phallus stretched the crotch of his trousers so much that it looked as if he was giving birth.

As tears of happiness fogged Megan's vision, she licked drops of Raymond's blood from her fingers. A feeling of deep love pervaded her being as she watched John's blood stained pants fall onto the plastic covered kitchen floor. Freed from its confinement, John's tail, with its little heart-shaped tips, twitched about frantically while he busied himself preparing her sandwich.

Megan watched her husband intently while he sautéed a large slice of Raymond's brain. She could hear it sizzling in the skillet. A sesame seed bun popped up from the toaster and bare assed John slathered it with mustard and horseradish.

With sandwich in hand, John slowly turned to face Megan and the sight of his leering grin, rigid manliness and steaming sandwich took her breath away. She stepped over Raymond's corpse and reached out to embrace her darling John. It was all just another beautiful reminder that Valentine's Day had come again.

THE SECRET SINNERS SOCIETY

"It was a torrential downpour. It happened so suddenly that I thought we were going to be hit by a tornado. The sky was swirling about, the wind was blowing and the rain was just pouring down. I had to crane my neck and strain my eyes to see though my fogged up windshield. The damn wipers could not keep up with the downpour and I worried that I was going to end up being in an accident with some fool before I got off of 69 North."

"While I'm peering out through my fogged up windows, I hear this loud bang and I'm sure two cars had just collided. Then my windshield starts to be streaked with red as my wipers begin to swish what looked like blood and pieces of flesh back and forth. In fact, most of my car was splattered with this stuff that sure as hell resembled blood and guts. I glanced to where the bang came from and saw this car with its hood all buckled in. The crumpled mess was also covered in stuff that looked like entrails and gore. My first thought was a deer must have jumped onto the car. I parked my car right there in the middle of 69, grabbed my umbrella, and hurried over to the car that had been hit to check on the driver. When I saw what laid there on the wet pavement, this pile of bloody pulp between my car and his, I almost vomited."

Tracey Collins first-hand account of the mysterious body that plummeted out of the sky onto Harlow Owen's car shocked residents of the Golden Triangle. The incident halted the evening commute for about five hours as police and other officials investigated the macabre scene on Highway 69, just north of Cooks Lake Road.

The victim, believed to be a man in his thirties, fell from a height high enough to cause his body to virtually explode on impact. News reports stated that the body had fallen at least 2000 feet. Pieces of it were strewn over a 25-yard radius according to one observer. Police cordoned off the crime scene and placed cones to mark off where each piece of the body had been found.

The news reports stated that the body crashed onto the hood of Harlow Owens' car about 5:45 pm. There was speculation that he might have been a drug dealer pushed from an aircraft or a helicopter, but at the time of the incident none of the witnesses remembered hearing or seeing any signs of a plane or helicopter flying above.

The deceased was identified by fingerprints as Raul Franklin, a small-time Beaumont, TX drug dealer and thug. Raul had a long rap sheet, but because of his guardian angel, attorney Bernie Pieper, he never saw the inside of a prison.

The officer in charge of the investigation of Raul Franklin's tragic death was Detective Richard Hancock. This was a case that Detective Hancock relished because for the last two years he'd been working cases involving Raul. Cases where Raul was a person of interest included three murders, eight rapes, illegal gambling, breaking and entering, car theft, robbery, being drunk and disorderly, and breaking the noise abatement laws. The last infraction was the one that had changed the nature of the investigation from just work to personal.

Before Raul's unfortunate death, he often enjoyed infuriating Detective Hancock by surreptitiously parking stolen cars right out in front of the detective's apartment and turning up the radio's volume full blast to serenade the sleeping occupants with the cacophonous, obnoxious, vile noise of rap. Detective Hancock's only recourse was to have the offending vehicles removed from the premise, which invariably took an hour or more. Often the cars turned out to be stolen property of well to do Beaumont residents that would have sued the police if their vehicles had been mishandled or damaged by the police to simply turn off the offending radio.

It was hard for Detective Hancock to conceal his joy as he looked down at the bloody corpse that was once the smug son-of-a-bitch motherfucker Raul Franklin. Old Bernie Pieper wasn't going to be much help to Raul this time.

Raul Franklin's death was never solved, and his case joined the unsolved crime files.

The mysterious death of Franklin wasn't the only unsolved murder in Beaumont that year; there was also the murder of Sheila Cushing, my mother. This unsolved case of who murdered my mother was probably the primary reason behind me becoming a cop. Being a woman cop is not the easiest job to have. You're looked down upon as physically weak, too emotional, burdened with too many female problems; bottom line, I'm seen as just a whole lot of extra baggage for my male partner. I was lucky; I was paired up with John Stein. He was a bookish, kind cop who desired to make a difference. We were the Beaumont Police Department's odd couple.

What follows is the story of my search for the truth behind the death of my mother, Sheila Cushing.

My mother was a young woman who ended up in Beaumont after a guy she'd hitchhiked from robbed and left her stranded. It was about two in the morning when she was unceremoniously shoved from the truck's cab and left barefooted on Martin Luther King Boulevard with just the clothes she was wearing. She watched tearfully as the truck's tail lights, her money, and meager possessions disappeared into the night. Finally Sheila pulled herself together and started walking down the deserted boulevard in the opposite direction that the truck had gone.

Vehicles occasionally zoomed by and honked, but no one stopped, and from the taunts and cat calls shouted at her, Sheila was probably lucky they hadn't.

After less than a mile her bare feet had become raw from the gravel and the road's abrasiveness, but the pain didn't stop her; she continued hobbling painfully on until a building festooned in lights came into view. In front, a big garish neon sign blinked out the words "Humpy's Strip Club, A

Gentleman's Nirvana."

As Sheila shambled onto its parking lot, a woman wearing a white leather micro skirt exited the club and strolled toward her vehicle. Sheila desperately cried out and the tall blonde stranger in four inch strappy heels suddenly stopped, gasped, and quickly clomped over to her. The woman steadied Sheila and muttered, "My God, what happened to you?"

The Good Samaritan's name was Angela Weeks, and this odd chance encounter became the beginning of their life-long friendship.

After Angela heard Sheila's blight, she invited her to stay at her apartment. The offer was tearfully accepted, and soon Sheila was sitting on Angela's living room couch smearing Neosporin all over her bloody feet. The two of them talked incessantly and a few hours before sunrise, Sheila finally fell asleep in the home of her Good Samaritan rescuer.

As Sheila soon discovered, her biggest problems were no ID or money. It seemed impossible to get a job without ID. She couldn't even dance at the strip joint because she couldn't prove her age.

Finally, as things worsened, Angela turned Sheila on to the appropriately named Big Top Escort Service. Sheila gravitated to her new life and loved the big money, the gifts, attention, and often even the sex. Men liked her, and she became immensely popular with her clients.

All of this about my mother, Sheila Cushing, would've never been known, if not for the seismological actions of my sex-crazed next door neighbors practicing the *suspended congress* Kama Sutra position. This crazy couple, with less brain cells than teeth, were doing this thing where the guy stands cradling the girl while she wraps her legs and arms around his body. He had her pressed up against our shared wall banging away at her like a jackhammer. It went on until the law of gravity trumped lust and a disk ruptured in his back and they collapsed to the floor. She broke her tail bone; he ruptured spinal disks, fractured his penis and tore open the urinary tube as his tool bent into a "V" as they fell.

Their bad luck was my good luck; their gyrations knocked most of the pictures off my side of the wall. One of those frames contained a photograph of my mother with two other people. When the glass and frame shattered, I pulled the photo from the debris and noticed writing on the back of it. The names were Sheila Cushing, Angela Weeks, and a guy just named Dick. Both my mother, Sheila Cushing, and Angela Weeks were kissing the cheeks of this guy named Dick.

I was living in Beaumont, TX when the infamous *suspended congress* attempt failed. In fact, that painful sex escapade actually coincided with my second year anniversary of being a Beaumont, TX police officer. I had no one in my life to celebrate the milestone with since at that time I was pretty much a perpetual loner. Celebrations had never been a mainstay of my life, so a glass of cheap wine and an early night to bed with my pink plastic buddy, Jack Rabbit Vibe, seemed quite adequate for the occasion.

I found it hard to sleep, and as the night progressed, the photo and the names printed on its reverse kept flitting back into my mind. Who were Angela Weeks and the hairy face guy named Dick? Those questions quizzed my inebriated mind until sleep finally overtook me.

At the police station the next day, I decided I'd make it my quest to discover who Angela Weeks was and if she was still alive and her current whereabouts. I wanted to know more about this old acquaintance of my mother. Hopefully, Angela would be able to tell me more about the mother I never really knew.

I had lost my mother by murder, according to my adoptive parents, but they never told me any real facts about her death and, for some macabre reason, I wanted to know more. I wanted to know about the investigation, who the suspects might have been, how was she killed, and where. Maybe some of what I wanted to know would be known by Angela Weeks.

The names on the back of the photo continued to intrigue me, and soon I was searching police records, news clippings, and Googling for anything I could find about this Angela Weeks. It wasn't long before I found an Angela Weeks from Beaumont, TX. She had numerous arrests for prostitution and a couple for bounced checks. She was also old enough to have known my mother. Most importantly, however was that her address was there in the police reports, so I decided to pay her an unofficial visit and see if she could tell me more about my mother and her story.

The same day I discovered the address of Angela Weeks, I drove out to it and found it to be in a rundown apartment building in one of the worst Beaumont neighborhoods. I parked down the street from it and watched who came and went. I sat there for almost an hour, but never spotted any woman who resembled Angela, or at least what I thought she'd look like this many years later. My stakeout, however, was interrupted when I got a call about a domestic dispute and had to roll. I vowed I'd visit Angela the next day, for real.

The next day I found myself walking the hallway of the apartment building looking for apartment 314. I found it and stood there questioning my sanity for coming. In my hand I held a copy of the only picture I had of my mother with Angela Weeks and the guy named Dick. I raised my hand a couple of times to knock on the door, but each time changed my mind; then I heard a group of young men bois- terously cursing and jiving coming up the stairs and decided if I was ever going to knock, I'd better do it now. It didn't take but a couple seconds before the door cracked open and a middle-aged woman peeked out. In a smoker's voice she said, "Yeah, what do you want?"

I held out a picture so the woman could see it through the opening and asked, "Is the woman on the right, you?

The woman moved closer to the opening and gasped "Oh my God; yes it is."

She looked back at me and said, "I know who you are. Sweet Jesus, you're Sheila's little girl. Oh my God, I can't believe it; you look so much like your mother." Tears started to flow.

"Can I come in and talk to you about my mother?"

Angela replied, "The place is a mess, but of course." The door swung open and she beckoned me in and slammed it closed just as four want-to-be gang bangers swaggered by asking if we wanted a good fucking.

The middle-aged woman held the picture in her hands and started to sob. "Your mother and I were the best of friends. She was so beautiful. She was such a fun person.

I still think of her all the time. I'm so sorry about what happened to your mother. Her death was so sad. I don't really want to talk about that time; it makes me just want to cry."

She held the picture out, looked at me, and said, "Look at you; little Paula, all grown up now, and you're the spitting image of your mother, you look so much like her. So how did you find me?"

"Well, first I need to tell you that my name is not 'Paula' anymore. My legal name is now, Karen Bickers. The Bickers were the family that adopted me. After they were killed, I decided I wanted to erase my past completely, so I changed Paula to Karen. I just felt that maybe Paula carried a bit of bad luck with it. So from now on please call me by Karen, okay?"

"So now to answer your question about how I found you."

"Well, a strange thing happened. That picture you have in your hands had been hanging on a wall in my apartment in a frame for years. Then just a couple of weeks ago it finally fell off the wall and shattered. When I pulled the photo from the broken glass, I saw your name on the back and decided I had to find you. The rest was easy. I'm a police officer, and your name was in our files."

At first she looked at me in a concerned way, but I reached out to hug her and she softened up again and started crying. "Really, I'm not here to harass you; I just want to know more about my mother."

I spent the next two hours with her. She told me how my mother and she met and how they struggled during the first few months of living together. She told me how much my mother loved me and how they both would take turns caring for me when I was a baby.

I told her that all I knew about my mother was that I lived with her for about two years before she was killed. I had always believed that my mother was a wonderful woman who was killed by some unknown person. That was the story my adoptive parents told me.

I finally got down to the other person in the picture, the young man with a lot of hair on his face. I asked her, "Who was this guy named Dick?"

Suddenly Angela's entire demeanor changed, and a look of fear spread across her face. For a couple of moments she just sat there saying nothing, but finally she said, "This is a very bad person, and it's best that you just forget him. He won't be able to help you know more about your mother."

"I deal with dangerous people every day. I'm a cop. Just tell me his real name and I'll never tell him who told me," I pleaded to Sheila.

"I'm sorry Karen, but I can't. Do you know that I probably have more pictures of your mom and, if you like, I'll try and find them and make you some copies; would you like that?"

I saw that she wasn't going to tell me anything about Dick, so I didn't push her anymore on that issue. I told her, "I'd love that."

I asked her the next nagging question about my mother; how was she killed.

Sheila fidgeted a bit and asked me, "Do you really want to know that?"

I replied, "Yes, I have wondered about her murder for years."

Sheila said, "How your mother was killed eats away at me every day. It was so gruesome, and there's just no way

I could sit here and tell you, her daughter, what happened. I'm sorry Karen. Maybe you should just read the police file on her death."

I felt foolish realizing that I had not done that already. I replied to Sheila, "You're right, I shouldn't expect you to tell me those details. I want to give you my cell phone number and, if you think of anything else you want to tell me about my mother, please call. Could I have your phone number also?"

Sheila gave me her cell phone number, and it was time for me to leave. We hugged, shed a couple more tears, and I left.

I drove around thinking about my mother, finally accepting the fact that she'd been a prostitute. It bothered me. It bothered me a lot, but what would I have done back then if I had no money, no ID, no nothing? I guess I might have done the same thing if that was the only way to survive. It dawned on me then that my father was probably one of her Johns. That bothered me even more.

While I was thinking about this, a call came in. A naked woman with a knife was reported to be in the mall's parking lot threatening others and totally psychotic.

When I got there, a crowd of people stood around her as she snarled and cursed them. She looked like she was maybe seventeen at the most. I wasn't in uniform, so I flashed my badge and told her I was a police officer and wanted to help her. Identifying myself as a police officer appeared to make her even more hysterical. She was just saying nonsensical things like, "Shit on your face. You bitch whore. Pig in your face. Jesus fuck your mother. Dick fuck you. I'll show you. I want to go home. Dick is bad."

I moved closer to her and said, "Please let me help you." Her eyes bulged out of her head and she held out her knife toward me, spat at me, and snarled like an animal. She kept on swearing and cursing at me. She must have been suffering from Tourette's syndrome and something else. Maybe she was schizophrenic?

I tossed her my jacket to put on, but she batted it away. She just continued with her rant, "Fuck jacket, my tits are beautiful. He's a bastard. Ugh! My legs spread for dick. Eeiyah, Dick is bad. Fuck like pig. He's my daddy. Daddy Dick is bad. Dick is bad. Go away. You smell like sweat. Daddy don't like sweat."

She started to do a little dance, undulating her hips while waving her knife around. People were clapping and cheering. She sort of smiled back at them. Her eyes bulged out more, then rolled up so only the white showed. I moved closer, but suddenly she buried the knife deep into her chest. She fell to the ground, spewing out, "Daddy Dick is bad. He's bastard. Daddy Dick!" Then there was silence except the gasp from the crowd. Just as she knifed herself, other officers and an ambulance arrived, but they were too late.

Her name was Bonnie Mae Philips. She was a runaway from Cobbtown, GA, a small town with a population of about 300. Before she ran away, Bonnie Mae had been living with her alcoholic mother and her mother's live-in boyfriend. Somehow, she ended up in Beaumont and made her living by being a street hooker. No one on the streets would tell me anything about her, like who she worked with or if she had a pimp. I heard some things like she was a wild one and got beat up a lot by some guy, but no one knew or would tell me who he was. He was white and maybe in his fifties was all I could get out of them.

At the office as I was writing up my report on the incident, I decided to pull the files on the unsolved case for my mother's murder.

Angela weeks was right; my mother's death was much more horrible than I had ever imagined, and I felt nauseous reading the report.

The forensic pathologist who performed the autopsy reported a presence of linear abrasions, tentative cuts on Sheila Cushing's wrist that may indicate suicidal tendency of the deceased. However, the brownish scab present on these linear abrasions suggested that they were inflicted two to three days prior to her murder.

Sheila Cushing suffered multiple blunt-force injuries to the head, neck, chest, abdomen, and vagina. The forensic evidence suggested that the beating was done just prior to the fatal stabbing.

The crime scene showed a great amount of blood on the deceased body, also a dry pool of blood on the bedspread, and more splattered on the bedroom walls and ceiling. Three severed fingers belonging to the deceased were found on the floor next to the bed.

All of her wounds were slit-like, consistent with a razor or sharp knife-like stabbing. Some of the wounds suggested that they were inflicted while Sheila Cushing was still alive. The three missing fingers indicated that Cushing tried to defend herself against her assailant. The wounds were found on her breast, abdomen, face, and one deep laceration through her thyroid cartilage into her trachea. No major blood vessels of the neck, however, were injured, but the large number of wounds caused exsanguination and hypovolemic shock that resulted in Sheila Cushing's death.

As I read the report, my body shuddered and my eyes flooded with tears, but I willed myself to cry silently. I did not want to attract any attention from other officers.

The investigating officer was Detective R. Hancock.

I wondered if that detective was now the Lieutenant Hancock who was my superior. Just as I was considering this possibility, another call came in for another domestic dispute out on Major Drive. I shoved the file about my mother's murder in a desk drawer and headed out with my partner, John Stein.

On the way out to Major Drive, I asked John about Lieutenant Hancock, like how long had Hancock been a cop. John told me that Hancock had been with the force for ages. He worked his way up through robbery, drugs, vice, homicide; you name it. He had a reputation of bending the rules a bit to get a perp. He even had the rat squad down on him a couple times, but Internal Affairs couldn't get anything to stick. He's a real hardened cop whom you don't get on the wrong side of. He has a lot of juice now, but they say he really had to overcome a lot of obstacles and wife problems to get to where he was.

I asked, "What were the obstacles he had to overcome?"

"His name mostly. A guy with a name with the word cock in it is bad enough, but when your first name is Richard and everyone is calling you Dick, that's really hard to overcome. It's rumored he punched a few officers out for calling him

Dick. Bottom line is, you never call him Dick to his face or to anyone because if it gets back to him, your life will be fucking miserable. You just refer to him as Lieutenant Hancock." I wanted to know more, but we arrived at the address of the altercation.

The complaint ended up as a couple just making too much noise for the neighbor who apparently called it in. We counseled the individuals to keep it down and not disturb their neighbors or we'd be back and have to make some arrests.

We called the disposition of the case as a 10-90F2 or a Domestic Incident Report of an unfounded report of domestic violence.

Back in the squad car John voiced his anger at racing out to these nuisance calls. He said, "Really a shame we have to play grownup to dumb ass grownups. There should be a special place for dumb asses to live, like an island for the tribe of dumb asses."

I agreed with him, and he continued on about something that Lieutenant Hancock used to do.

Talking about the LT reminded John that Hancock used to come out to these projects on Christmas all dressed up in his medieval costume with some of his reenactor buddies. John said, "They would all be dressed up in costume and riding horses, like a page out of Robin Hood. His name with the group of reenactors as you could guess was Sir Richard. He's a big shot with their crowd also. It was a big show for the kids. Even some of the gang bangers were impressed. They would give toys and food to the younger kids. He can be a good guy sometimes... He loves to help kids. He has a soft heart for kids who get stuck being children of drug addicts, whores, and alcoholics."'

"Who is this medieval crowd you're talking about?"

"Oh it's some reenactor group up north of Silsbee," John replied.

"I think that would be fun being a member of a group like that. I might just check them out."

John said, "Well, be careful being one of those wenches or vixens of old, because good old Lieutenant Hancock is also known as being a ladies' man. They say that when he was in vice he used to test the wares a bit and that almost got him divorced."

"Thanks for the warning. Maybe I'll just stay my old boring self then."

I didn't have to ask Angela who the hairy faced guy named Dick was; I now knew who he was. It was Richard Hancock when he was simply a detective or an officer, but a bit of doubt still lingered in my mind. Maybe I was just making all these assumptions just to try and get quick closure. There was one sure way to find out if Richard Hancock was the man in the photograph. I'd visit Angela Weeks again.

Later that night I called Angela and told her I had something else I wanted to show her. She said she couldn't do it that evening, but lunch at her apartment the following day would be okay. She also cautioned that it was best that our visits weren't known to other cops.

All night long I kept thinking about this strange turn of events, my mother's forensic report, and that poor naked girl dancing about and its bloody aftermath. I still found it hard to deal with blood and gore. All and all, it was a very traumatic day.

The next morning I had preliminary forensic reports on Bonnie Mae Philips. I quickly perused the report to see if she was on some drug that made her lose it and kill herself. She was such a pretty girl. There was no mention of drugs, but I did find it interesting that she had three scabbed over cuts on her right wrist. Maybe she'd been trying to commit suicide for the last few days. It was obvious that she was suicidal along with a few other psychological problems. She also had deep teeth marks on her ass.

The report said the bites weren't typical bites of passion, but very deep bites where a small piece of skin was torn loose by the perpetrator. The area of the bite hadn't healed and was seriously infected. The bite would have caused serious pain. The bite mark analysis indicated that the perpetrator of this act was missing the lower left central incisor. It was odd, but thinking of someone biting me like that made me shudder. Was it a lover who went crazy and bit her so hard to hurt her or was it some sick John who just enjoyed hurting and marring women?

I worked more on my Bonnie Mae Philips incident report and watched the clock so I wouldn't be late for my meeting with Angela.

I left the station house at eleven and bought a bouquet of flowers for Angela. I was betting it wasn't often that she received flowers.

Angela was seriously surprised at the flowers and displayed a huge smile of appreciation. I noticed that she had a puffy lip on the left side of her face and asked her what happened. She replied, "It's just part of the life of being a hooker. You know? I never thought I'd end up like this, but here I'm, an old worn out hooker."

I didn't know how to reply so I just hugged her.

Through a little sob she said, "I think I'm going to like having you as a friend." She hugged me back hard.

She pushed me away and said, "Sit down, I made us lasagna. I hope you like lasagna; it was your mother's favorite. So what do you want to show me?"

I pulled out a newspaper clipping that I had and handed it to her.

I asked if she knew who was in the picture. She stood transfixed, then suddenly threw the clipping back at me. She said in a frightened voice, "I told you to forget trying to find Dick, but you didn't listen, and now, girl, you're in for some serious problems, along with me. I hadn't had contact with that bastard for years."

Angela was breathing heavy, and her eyes darted around the room like she was looking for something.

"Have you talked to him? Have you?"

I quickly replied, "No Angela. No one knows except you and me. I wasn't totally sure that Dick was Lieutenant Richard Hancock, until now. Why is this such a bad thing?"

"Are you dense Karen? He's, he is the bastard who killed your mother." Her statement transfixed me. Her voice sort of faded away, but kept repeating in my head.

"If he knows what you know, he'll kill you. Just go out on the street and ask about him. He's a monster."

I just sat in my chair and stared at Angela. "Lieutenant Hancock killed my mother?" My voice came out in almost a whisper.

Angela moved over to me, and hugged me, and softly said, "Yes, the bastard did."

"Why did he kill my mother?"

Angela hesitated, then replied, "Because he wanted your mother to stop seeing other men, but she wouldn't. She needed the money. He wasn't giving her a dime, and she didn't know any other way to support the two of you. One day he caught her coming in way late, and he could tell she'd been with someone. That started a huge fight. She tried to make him leave, but he wanted to punish her. He punched her a few times, once hard in the face, but she wouldn't stop telling him she was going to do whatever she damned well pleased."

Angela continued, "Richard couldn't take a woman yelling back at him, especially a woman he considered a whore. Suddenly he pulled a folded up straight razor out of the inside of a cowboy boot. He threatened her with it and she still didn't back down. She should've, because then he went insane and just started to slash her with the razor. She screamed and you woke up. She called him crazy and begged him to go.

"That was when I ran to your crib and tried to comfort you. Your mother kept screaming, then suddenly I could only hear that bastard swearing and puffing as he cut her even more. He went totally berserk.

"He came into your bedroom with his sweaty face splattered with your mother's blood and I begged him not to kill us. You were crying so loud as if you knew what had just happened. He made me put you back in the crib, then he dragged me out to the living room. He grabbed my hair and forced me to look at your dead mother. He pushed my face right down into your mother's face and told me I'd end up carved like a turkey if I ever said anything about what happened to your mother. To show me he was serious he sliced my arm with his razor. Right here on my wrist."

I looked at her outstretched arm and could see three faint white lines where the cuts had healed over.

Angela continued, "I believed him then and I still believe him now that if I told, he'd slice me to death just like he did your mother. He made me help roll your mother's corpse up in a shower curtain and a rubber sheet from your crib. He made me leave you in the bed by yourself while we rode over to Folsom Street and put your mother's body into a trash bin. She wasn't found for five more hot July days. The news reports said a sanitation worker saw her body fall out of the trash container and into the garbage truck as he was emptying it. Before he could turn off the hydraulics, her body was crushed by the compactor.

"Who do you think was first on the scene? That fucking Detective, Dick Hancock.

"Your mother's body was so disfigured and decomposed by the time it was discovered that we had to have a closed casket funeral for her. Even then the bastard couldn't leave her alone. He showed up at the funeral pretending to be searching for a possible suspect. Anyway, I'm sure you've read the report on your mother's death. It was never solved. The news kept reporting that the murderer was believed to be some psycho killing prostitutes."

I asked her, "Why are you telling me all this now?"

"Because if you talked to others, he'd know you'd talked to me and he'd kill me and probably you. He does not intend to ever be caught."

She paused for a moment and added, "I think he's killed others also. He's a man with no conscience or remorse.

"I'd also be an accessory to the crime because I helped clean up the crime scene and moved your mother's body. I lied to other officers who were investigating and helped protect Hancock. I'd go to prison also."

The accusations from Angela bored into my head and I kept thinking horrible thoughts about what I wanted to do to that bastard Richard Hancock. Slowly my thoughts of hate turned to thoughts of revenge, then I discovered I was actually planning his death. He'd die for what he did to my mother. I'd kill him. He took my mother's life, and all I wanted now was to see him beg for his life. I fantasized about taking a straight razor and cutting a furrow into his chest, then watching the skin pop open as the blood oozed out. He'd scream, then I'd cut another furrow next to the last one. He'd beg and scream some more, then I'd take pliers and push them into the furrows I had cut into his chest and slowly tear out chunks of flesh from his chest. He'd scream and scream, but that's what I'd want. I'd want him to suffer. I wanted to cut him up with a straight razor and make his death as excruciating as my mother's had been.

I'd kill him, but I had to figure out how and where so I wouldn't be caught. I had to hide my hate because every day I had to see him at the station.

A week after I discovered that he killed my mother, I received a cryptic note in my mailbox inviting me to become a member of some obscure organization called the Secret Sinners Society of Texas. At first I thought it was a joke, but later that night I received a call from an elderly sounding man who confirmed that such a group existed and that I was truly invited to join it. I had vaguely heard about this group a few times before, but had dismissed it as some fairy tale. The anonymous caller said the purpose for the group was to provide a supportive ear to people who had secrets and cursed with a strong yearning to reveal them to someone. The caller said I was invited to meet one of its oldest members in person the following evening at a Beaumont restaurant. He warned me that at that meeting I'd be asked to carry out an unethical act as my initiation into the group. I could refuse and nothing would come of it, but if I agreed to the deed, it was to remain a secret from everyone accept the members of the local Secret Sinners Society of Texas. I'd be free to tell them about my deal at one of the meetings if I so desired.

After all that had happened to me, I must have been weak because I agreed to meet with this man.

The next evening was emotional; part of me told me not to go, but my curiosity kept pushing me on. Part of me kept telling me I'm a cop, I have a gun, I can protect myself if things get weird, but an inner voice reminded me that I had secrets with lots of sin, and it'd be nice to tell someone who wasn't going to judge me. Then suddenly, I found myself sitting in the parking lot of the Beaumont Grill totally confused as to what to do. I sat there maybe three or four minutes before I finally exited the car into the warm Texas evening. I wasn't sure what I was even looking for other than I was supposed to be meeting an old man.

I entered the lobby and felt my face flush with embarrassment as I told the young hostess that I was supposed to be meeting an older gentleman with an oxygen tank. She seemed to know immediately who I was referring to and grabbed a menu and motioned me to follow. We entered one of the dining rooms and I saw a man with a head engulfed in silvery white hair and an oxygen tank next to his chair. He reminded me of Colonel Sanders because he was dressed in white and had this bushy beard that hid part of his face and neck. He also sported a droopy mustache that hung like some flaccid hairy appendage under his nose. He wheezed a kindly welcome as I took the seat opposite of him.

I immediately felt misgivings for being there, and he sensed my uneasiness because he reached out and patted my hand and said, "Don't be nervous."

He poured himself some wine and beckoned me to do the same. "So I bet you'd like to know more about our nice little social group," he said in a teasing way?

I nodded yes as I stared into his gray eyes.

He replied, "Okay! Well then, first you'd be joining a very select number of individuals who, like you, have secrets that eat away at them. They want to tell someone, because that's our nature. You do something extraordinary; you just want to tell the world, but you can't, if what you did was, let's say, not that ethical or just downright illegal. I guess you could say we're our own therapy group. Our meetings keep us sane and let us brag a little about our deeds or get a degree of relief from unburdening ourselves from some dark secret that society would never understand. Our group doesn't cast stones because we know we're all a bunch of sinners.

We laugh at your deeds, cry with you about your sins, and sometime even celebrate your wrong doing. We don't care what you did. Regardless of how despicable your act was, we don't judge. But we do have rules."

He let that last statement just hang there for a long moment. Maybe he was waiting for me to ask him what the rules were. So I asked, "What are the rules?"

He looked again at me with his gray eyes and said, "Our only rule is that you can never repeat any tale you heard from a member of our unique little society."

The old man bent over the table and whispered, "Members who break that rule are never forgiven, and bad things happen to them and their families. Very, very bad things."

He paused for a moment to let the warning sink in, then leaned back into his seat, "We'd love to have you as a member. I think you'd find our engagements very stimulating and entertaining."

He paused again, then continued, "The only requirements for you to join is to simply say yes and perform one little unethical act that would serve as your initiation into our group. Would you like to hear what that would be?"

He had me hooked. I couldn't think of anything bad that I wanted to talk about, but I sure as hell wanted to hear about these other confessions. Some might even solve crimes I was working on. I said, "Let's hear what the task is."

He winked at me and again leaned over the table a bit so he could talk quietly. He wanted me to impersonate someone in his evil plan to ruin the reputation and marriage of a cop. A part of me hoped that he'd tell me it was Richard Hancock that I was supposed to destroy... The person turned out to be someone equally as disgusting and actually a cop I knew and loathed. I again had a strong desire to just get up and leave, but some deep intuition told me that it would be alright to join and be a part of this strange organization. My mind raced wondering if this Colonel Sanders look alike was an old cop and if all the members were cops.

The old man explained what I had to do and, upon finishing his instructions, he told me to call him when I had completed the tasks. I told him I would, if I had his number. I actually laughed a bit about what he'd asked me to do. While I was laughing he pressed into my hand a business card with nothing on it except a phone number.

Later that evening I made the call with a cell phone he'd also given me.

I dialed the number and a woman quickly answered. I greeted her with, "Hello, Mrs. Williams?"

"Yes, and who am I talking to?" she responded.

I braced myself and said, "You don't know me, but your fucking cheating husband does, and he got me pregnant and gave me gonorrhea."

Mrs. Williams interrupted, "You must be calling the wrong Williams. My husband is a cop and doesn't mess around with anyone. I'm sorry about your situation, but you have the wrong number."

"Mrs. Williams, if your husband's first name is Edward, has 'The South will rise again' tattooed above his dick, and his ass has a scar from where he took a bullet, then I got the right wife. I'm just trying to help you. And I'm a little upset that he got me pregnant. He told me he was fixed. The lying bastard."

"Oh my God! That fucking prick. How long has he been, ugh, with you?"

I replied, "He's been dating me for about two years and told me he was leaving you, but now that I'm pregnant, I see that was a big lie. He doesn't want to divorce you because it will cost too much he said."

"That bastard. He's been sleeping with you for two years?"

"Not only me; Edward said he's been sleeping with two other women besides me."

She kept repeating as I told her the story, "That bastard, that fucking bastard."

I continued with my story. "When I asked Edward who the other women were, he wouldn't tell me. Maybe one was you and who knows who the other might be. What I do know is that I hadn't been sleeping around, so he picked up the case of gonorrhea from you or some other woman or hell, who knows, maybe he was plugging some boys also. He's a little dandy sometimes."

She screamed over the phone, "I swear, if I have gonorrhea, I'll kill him. I'll fucking kill him."

I interjected at that point, "Sweetie, you need to visit the Jefferson County Health Clinic and help them stop old drippy dicks VD epidemic. I hate to bring up another issue, but we need to talk about child support and money for me to have your husband's baby. I need thirteen thousand dollars just for the hospital stay."

Suddenly Mrs. Williams yelled, "Fuck you! I'm not giving you one red cent, you fucking whore. I'm going to kill your

Goddamn fucking bastard of a boyfriend and sweetie don't ever call here again."

The phone clicked off, and I started to laugh at what I had done. Detective Edward Williams was toast. He wasn't going to talk his way out of this because he really did have clap from fucking a prostitute that the health department had warned the police about. Instead of arresting her, the vice cops gave her a free pass if she'd spend a night or two with Williams. He was stupid enough to sleep with her, and now he was suffering from the drips.

I didn't learn till much later why they wanted me to do this. Edward had apparently bedded a couple wives of other officers and got one pregnant. You can't do things like that in a small town's police department without making a lot of enemies. It was time for payback, and I was the weapon to get him punished. A video of his lovemaking with the diseased harlot had also been made and surreptitiously dropped off on the Police Chief's desk.

The old man was right; doing these types of things just made you want to tell someone. I was now a pledged member of the Texas branch of the Secret Sinners Society, and I looked forward to being invited to their get together just so I could tell my story to them.

Later that night I was watching a Sweeney Todd rerun and an ad caught my attention. It was a replica of the Sweeney Todd straight razor complete with a leather barber strop. It was a beautiful razor, made from stainless steel, an actual collector's piece. I was tempted to call the one eight hundred number and thought better of it. I needed to buy the murder weapon from a garage sale or antique shop with cash, but I knew a straight razor was what I'd use to carve that son of a bitch up with. I wanted to be like Bad, Bad Leroy Brown, the baddest man in the whole damn town. I could just envision the furrows opening on his chest as the blade sliced deep.

At work now I became much more observant of Richard Hancock. I learned everything about him, and strangely, I felt he was actually taking a liking to me. He seemed to accidentally bump into me and greeted me more. Then one day he cornered me at the bulletin board and asked if I was up to grabbing a couple drinks with him after our shift.

I was shocked, but kept my cool, and my dark side replied, "Yes, sure I'd love to."

He added that our rendezvous had to be kept quiet in the station.

Richard met me at a place called Alibis right off Interstate 10 in Beaumont, TX. It was dark and a bit dreary. It also had strippers and waitresses who revealed just about every inch of their skin.

I felt terribly nervous sitting across the table from the murderer of my mother in some strip joint, but I was unwavering in my plans to kill the bastard. What was that saying; keep your friends close and your enemies even closer. I wanted Richard really close. I watched him intently. He looked a bit nervous also as he held his glass of beer in front of him. His wedding ring shone as he tapped his finger quietly on the rim of the glass and occasionally pulled at little tuffs of hair that grew on the back of his ring finger.

Our waitress, Pearl, returned, bringing Richard another beer and a message from the next dancer. She told Richard that Celeste, the dancer, wanted him to know that his new bimbo didn't look like she had what it takes to work the pole. I guess she was talking about me because the dark eyed dancer leered at me as she wriggled up and down the chrome-plated pole. Her bulbous breasts seemed to circle the pole on their own volition. I glared back at this piece of trash and could feel my anger building up. She was insulting with her taunting vulgar stare. She was like some evil snake slithering up and down the pole, twisting herself in obscene ways. She'd bend her head down so her darting tongue would wet her hard nipples. I wanted to hurt her, she was so slutty, but I knew I had to stay focused on killing Richard.

He noticed the change in my demeanor and said, "Hey, don't let Celeste get to you; she's jealous of all women. The way she is, you wouldn't think she was a day over thirty, but she's 48 years old?

Suddenly she dropped from the pole to the stage floor and locked her legs behind her head. She spun around on her back like a flipped turtle. She came to rest with her posterior pointing straight at us. She proceeded to rock herself back and forth with her crotch looking like it was trying to eat its way through the micro thong that barely covered her vagina.

I turned to Richard and asked, "Why did you invite me to this shit hole? I'm not into sitting around watching a spinning tuna taco. Why are we here?"

"Wow! I like this place. I have friends here, but I understand Celeste bothers you. I just thought you might like to kick back like most of the rest of the guys and relax a bit with a beer or two. This is one of those places where the bad guys and the good guys both hang out with an unspoken agreement that we don't jack with each other while we're here. Anyway, I wanted to see how things have been going for you at the station. Can I help you on anything? I'm just trying to be friendly."

I looked at him and said, "Just how friendly are you trying to get?"

"I'm a gentleman, especially with female officers. I don't think you feel any tentacles feeling you up, do you?"

I smiled at him and said, "Your wife knows you fuck around?"

"We're not fucking around, so why are you asking me that? You and I are just here talking shop. How is the Bonnie Mae Philips case going?"

I looked at him and smiled. "Sure, Richard we're just talking shop in a sleazy strip joint where I bet you've fucked everyone here. The case is going fine; I'm trying to get more info on the girl's background."

"Is it worth all this work? She was an unfortunate hooker who killed herself, so why all the drama?"

He smiled, and in the dim light I noticed that he had a missing tooth on his lower jaw. A chill ran through my body as I wondered if it was Richard who had bit that girl. "Daddy Dick," was what she kept repeating? Was he Daddy Dick?

Richard kept tossing out a bunch of pickup lines, but finally he gave up and said, "Maybe someday in the future we could go out on a real date." The sleaze bag continued, "You do like dating older men, correct? Cause I never see you with anyone your age."

"I just don't date period," I fired back.

We both were pretty drunk from the gallons of beer they kept putting on our table and finally I told him, "I'm going home, alone."

He looked at me and said, "That's fine. Go home. I hate being with girls who puke when you poke them. We can get together another night." That was it for that evening.

Saturday evening the meeting for the Secret Sinner's Society was to be held in the living room of a bed and breakfast called the Book Nook Inn. The place was located just outside of Beaumont, TX. The event was a masquerade party, and everyone attending had to wear a mask and stay in costume during the entire affair. In fact, every meeting of the Secret Sinners Society required members attend their function in costume.

The masquerade party was more of a lavish affair than I had ever envisioned. Whoever was responsible for this odd get together had catered food delivered to the Inn. A large table had been set up in one section of the Inn's large living room, allowing all of us to sit together. There were twelve of us in total. Apparently we had the entire Inn to ourselves. A person who others called "Insider" stated that the Inn had been cleared of all recording and surveillance devices, but just in case, two boom boxes were employed to blast rock and roll music to make recording conversation even more difficult.

They named me the "Voice." Everyone had to have a handle of some type and, if I didn't like my nickname, I could rename myself later.

The Insider told the rest that the "Voice" had an interesting story to tell about a cop who was no more. All the masked faces turned toward me and I could see the eyes staring at me. I smiled beneath my Afghan burqa that hid my face and enveloped my body. I told this group my story of how I destroyed Detective Edward Williams.

Talking about it, or maybe I should say bragging about it, made me feel a little upbeat.

It's awful to admit that doing evil things could actually be exhilarating, but I think it does and brings about a catharsis of the being. I hoped that when I kill Richard, his death would clear away all the hate that was eating away at me.

A few more stories were told, and one was interesting, about a guy who discovered his wife cheating with one of his best friends. He actually bought her lingerie and rubbed it in poison ivy before he wrapped it up for her. It was a sexy crotchless teddy that he hoped she'd wear for her next rendezvous with her lover. Apparently she did, and the moisture and heat they produced grinding their loins together caused the poison ivy oil to spread all over their genitals.

He said his wife had it even inside her vagina, and its lips swelled so bad that they looked like two red bananas stuck to her crotch oozing with pus. He quipped, "If you filled her ginormous labia with helium she'd have floated up and away. She couldn't even wear panties for over a week."

He said, "Her boyfriend couldn't go to work because his penis was so swollen and burning that he had to lie in bed for three days with his legs spread wide. Whenever he pissed he could barely touch his penis because it burnt so bad."

More wine and beer flowed as another told his rollicking story of sin, sex, and a little gore. Laughter punctuated the story, and ten minutes later another round of applause was given for this guy's tale. These were much more uglier tales than mine. I wondered how long clubs like these had been going on.

After his delivery and one more tale of woe, the most interesting one was told. This man telling the story was referred to as "Pogo." His tale was about a man whom he'd hated for years. Finally the torment he endured from this bastard pushed him to the breaking point where he justly decided to exact his revenge.

Pogo said, "This drug dealer; a fucking piece of human excrement kept fucking with me until I finally had no choice but to kidnap the creep. The bastard had it coming. He'd killed numerous others with a gun, beaten others to death with his hands, and many more died from the shit he was selling on the street. So I felt pretty good about it when I kidnapped him. I really did. I took him to this place in the Big Thicket north of Beaumont, TX where we could be real private. I beat the shit out of him first. In fact, I broke in a brand new Rawlings baseball bat. A damn good bat for that kinda work. It was the kind of bat that doesn't break when you're banging on someone's kneecap."

Pogo continued, "Man, I swung the bat so hard that I broke the bastard's arms. He had bones sticking out through his skin. The guy's legs were so badly mangled that, when I moved him, it looked like he had five or six knees instead of one.

"I had one more big surprise for him, I had created a device that was sort of like the catapult of old and had mounted it in the bed of my truck. Anyway, I dragged that fucking drug dealer over to the truck, pulled him up onto the catapult's bucket. I draped his broken legs and arms over it sides. I brought him back to consciousness with some smelling salts. The minute he came to, he started screaming in agony. I wanted to tell him again why he was in this situation, but he just couldn't stop screaming from the pain or sobbing.

"He lay on his back looking up at me with snot and blood glistening all over his face and chest. I tried to talk to him, but he wouldn't stop his sniffling and yelling in pain. Finally I told him, "I'm going to try and send you up to heaven. If they like you, they'll keep you, but if not, you'll be returned to earth with a big bang."

"I waved a big straight razor around in front of his face and he started to whimper and begged me not to hurt him anymore. I looked at this pathetic pile of shit, then brought the razor down fast through the middle of his stomach, splitting it wide open. His guts sprung out of him like old Jackie out of the box. I pulled the release lever on the catapult, and he went flying with his entrails trailing behind him like the tail of a kite. He flew up over the trees still yelling. That was the last I heard or saw of that bastard."

As Pogo told his story I noticed him habitually picking at the small tuffs of hair on the back of his left hand and suddenly a strange stirring moved within my gut as his identity came to me. This recognition felt like something had crawled up inside of me; something vile and putrid. Even my heart raced like I had just ran five miles.

Under the shroud of my burqa, sweat poured from my pores, but my body felt like ice. The laughter and applause filled the room as I sat silent, shocked that I knew who "Pogo" was. It was Richard Hancock!

I wondered if the razor he'd used on this guy was the same one he'd used on my mother. Like Angela had said, he liked razors and cutting people. I took some deep breaths and bit down hard on my lip to gain control. Finally the world outside my burka came into focus again.

I was glad that I was wearing something that hid my face because I'd have given away my emotions, I'm sure.

How life had thrust this murderer back into my life was beyond mere coincidence; it was like destiny. It was my mother calling out and leading me to the fiend who took her life. She wanted revenge. Maybe she'd knocked the picture off the wall that had Dick's picture to tell me who sliced her up and dumped her in the garbage. I trembled with anger under the burka as these thoughts filled my mind. I looked forward to killing him and seeing him suffer. Thankfully, Pogo, or Richard Hancock, didn't speak again and about an hour later the get-together concluded.

That night I could not hardly sleep, but my plans began to take shape. I'd seduce that bastard and get him to take me someplace secret and kill him there. I wanted his wife to suffer also. I wanted her to know what kind of bastard she'd married. It wouldn't take much to seduce him, he was already showing interest in me. I wondered if he recognized me at the meeting. He didn't appear to, but he was also probably good at being deceptive.

Two days later I saw him in the corridor of the station and walked by him, gave him a big smile and a little girly wave of my hand. About thirty minutes later he was knocking on my office door holding a bunch of folders. I told him to come in and he said he was looking over the files again about the

Bonnie Mae Philips suicide. He asked if I was done with my investigation. I told him no, then asked, "So is your wife back, Richard?"

He smiled and said, "Matter of fact, she's not."

"So maybe you should show me your castle while she's away." I smiled up at him. My brashness caught him off guard, and he sort of stuttered momentarily, then said, "I was thinking the same thing. Let me give you the address and, if you come over at seven, I'll treat you to Chef Hancock's Italian special, an elegant dinner for two at my place."

I gave him a big thank you look, then just gazed up into the bastard's face and said, "I'll be there, Richard." I paused for a moment, then said, "I don't think we should be seen together here talking too much. We don't need rumors. Maybe you should make a little noise about my incomplete report on the Bonnie Mae Philips case so no one would suspect that we're seeing each other. We're seeing each other now, right?"

He displayed a sheepish grin and said, "You're a smart girl and that's a good idea. We certainly don't need my fucking wife getting a sniff of this. I'll give you a good ass chewing tomorrow morning at the shift meeting." In a lower voice he leaned over and quipped, "And maybe a much more personal ass chewing sometime real soon and winked at me."

His remark made me think about the large hunk of flesh ripped out of Bonnie Mae Philips's ass cheek, but as disturbing as that vision was, I maintained my coquettishness. He didn't fumble the ball; he wanted me over that night. As he exited my office and closed the door I realized that something outside of my control, something supernatural, something from the dark side, was orchestrating all of this. I was just a player in this deadly drama unfolding before me.

Before I went to Richard's home, I visited Angela and told her what was going on. I needed her to know where I was going, in case I disappeared. Even more important, I needed her to call me and give me an excuse to leave Richard's house at a certain time. I told her that I'd call or text her and five minutes later she should call me and tell me that she'd just been diagnosed with breast cancer and needed me to come and comfort her. I changed her name on my phone to a Nancy Hanna so Richard wouldn't accidentally see the name Angela pop up on my phone.

Angela expressed her concern for my safety being alone with Richard and begged me not to go, but those dark forces within me told me to go.

I arrived at Richard's house wearing a seductive black mini dress with a single loose fitted sleeve. It had a large cut out on the left side that I was sure would entice this pervert even more. On the way over I stopped and picked up a bottle of wine for a house gift. I hoped I could keep up the act long enough to figure out how I could kill him and get away with it. This night wasn't going to be the night, but his death was right around the corner.

Richard answered the door almost before I rang the bell, and I could see from his reactions that he liked my dress. He invited me in, escorted me to the living room, and asked if I'd like a drink. I was wary of him giving me something in the drink, so I demanded that we drink my wine instead and that I pour for us. He acquiesced to my demand, and a minute or so later we were toasting friendship. I was surprised at myself how well I was able to act so nonchalant when, inside, hatred was ripping me apart. I complimented him on his home and asked him to give me the grand tour of the place. We went by one door and he passed right by it. I asked where does that door go and he replied, "To the garage. There's nothing to show you there accept my motorcycle and grease stains." I feigned interest in the motorcycle and said, "I'd love to see it; maybe we could go on a ride on it soon. I love them."

Richard perked up a bit and said, "Okay! Let's take a look then. We stepped into the garage, and I quickly scanned the gloom to see what else might be there. There weren't any bodies or chains hanging from rafters; in fact, the garage was neat. Richard, or his wife, was apparently one of those neat nuts that everything had to be in its proper place. On the wall hung an armored suit along with a few ancient weapons displayed over what looked like a mini catapult. I hesitated at first to ask what the contraption was, but then decided to walk closer to it and ask instead about the weapons on the wall. He named the weapons. He had war axes, lances, pikes, spiked maces, swords, scythes, and lots of other old weapons.

Finally I pointed to the mini catapult and asked, "What's this thing?"

He said it was his new and improved 21st century catapult. I asked, "Is this one of those things that can fling huge rocks up into the air and into a castle?"

He said, "Yes," and added, "For its size it's more powerful than those of medieval times. This one used a combination of large flat springs and powerful coiled springs with an electric wench motor to actually set the catapult. The wench motor pulls down the bucket attached to a steel arm until the arm is almost parallel with the base of the catapult. When the brake of the wench is released, the bucket shoots forward, throwing whatever is in it 300 or 400 yards. That's a distance equivalent to about three football fields."

He said, "I used this quite often at functions with my medieval reenactment group up in Silsbee, TX. We shoot watermelons, buckets of rotting tomatoes and harmless stuff like that in our displays, but in medieval times, besides using it for attacking fortresses with boulders and flaming debris, they also flung horse manure, diseased dead animals, and even human bodies back into the castles being sieged."

"My catapult is also mobile. I can load the entire machine into the bed of my truck. That's something they would have loved back 800 years ago."

I envisioned Richard using this thing on the drug dealer. It actually gave me goose bumps on my arms as I thought about it. Richard interrupted my thoughts when he asked, "Are you ready to eat?"

I told him, "Yes!"

We returned to his dining room and he told me to sit down and he'd bring on the appetizers and some more wine. I told him while you're getting the appetizers I need to use the bathroom. Once in the bathroom, I texted Angela and reminded her to call me in five minutes. I erased my text message before returning to the table.

We again toasted to friendship, and I tried his Tomato-Basil Crostini and Prosciutto-Wrapped Fennel. I had to admit, he was a good cook even if he was the murderer of my mother. I praised him more about his house and asked him more questions about his reenactment group. I told him it sounded like a lot of fun being a member. I asked if it would be possible for me to join or would that complicate things too much. While he told me how much fun it would be if I was a member, my thoughts were off visiting something entirely different. I was wondering how often a killer gets to sit across from her victim and just chit chat with them before they take their life.

I felt a strong sense of control now because I knew he trusted me and that I lacked any feelings for the pain I'd soon inflict on him. Just then, as I was envisioning him begging for mercy in my mind, my phone rang. It was Angela, and she did an excellent job of pretending to be a woman in terrible distress because of her pending mastectomy. I held my hand over the phone and whispered to Richard that I was sorry, but I had to go and console my friend. I told him, "We'll have to do this another night real soon before your wife returns."

Richard said, "I understand. No problem. These things happen. Go take care of your friend and we'll continue this another day."

I left his house feeling upbeat, thinking what I'd soon be doing to him crystallizing in my mind. He only had a couple more days left in this world, and soon he'd be roasting in hell with others who beat and killed women.

I returned to Angela's apartment and told her how things went. She suggested that I return to his house and finish it since he was all alone that night. I didn't like spur of the moment ideas with something as serious as killing someone, but I wanted to get it over with. It was time he died. It would be great for his wife to come home and find her sweet little husband gone from this world. I tossed the idea around in my mind for awhile, then agreed that tonight was the night to kill the bastard.

I needed to get one thing from my house, so I returned to it, and while I was there called Richard from my cell phone. I told him the crisis with Nancy was over, and if he'd like, I could return and finish dinner unless it was too late. Of course he told me to come back.

I put my barber's razor in my purse along with another bottle of wine and headed out to his house again. The realization that I wouldn't be seeing him in the corridors of the police station ever again made me smile. His disappearance would be a blessing to a lot of other cops besides me.

Richard met me at the door with a big smile. He ushered me in and suddenly gave me a hug. I told him to slow down a bit. I smiled coyly at him and said that I had a present for him.

We went into the living room and sat on the couch. I told Richard that I had a little gift for him, but I don't want him to see it till I tell him he can look. He whined about that, then finally conceded. I took a pair of panties out of my purse and told him I had to wrap them around his eyes so he couldn't peek. He laughed and said sure, go right ahead and wrap your panties around my head. He kept trying to peek so I wrapped them tightly around his eyes.

I told Richard to keep his eyes closed and put his hands together, palms up, on the coffee table. I told him to get ready for a nice big surprise. I reached back into my purse and pulled out the razor. I kept smiling and blowing in his face, ears, and did a little cooing.

Suddenly I swung the open barber's blade down across his fingers. He gasped, and said "What the hell, that hurt," then suddenly he realized his fingers were gone. He reached up to his face with the bloodied stumps of his hands and pushed the panties away from his eyes. He stared at his fingerless hands and shrieked, "Jesus Christ, you cut all my fingers off."

I smiled and replied, "Not quite Dicky," as I swung the razor one more time and felt it connect with his left thumb. It sliced through it like it was a piece of celery.

"You're fucking insane," he yelled and tried to smash in my face with his elbow, but he missed. His action made him lose his balance and he crashed to the floor. Blood was getting everywhere. His face was streaked like an Indian with red war paint where he'd brushed the panties away from his eyes. Richard glistened with his own blood.

Suddenly I felt another presence in the room. It was cold, and I think it gave off an odor like maybe sewer gas. I couldn't see it, whatever it was, but I knew it was near. In fact, I began to feel like I was looking through a mist. This strange feeling was so strong that it frightened me more than what I was doing to Dick. My thoughts were interrupted by Dick whining, "Why are you doing this?"

I told him, "Stay on the floor or I'll Taser your balls next. I want to look into your eyes and see the fear of your upcoming death." As I said that, my whole body convulsed like something or someone was shaking me. My skin blossomed with goose bumps, and my throat burnt from the bile that had suddenly filled my mouth. The strange presence was even stronger now, but I fought it. It was something dark returning to me again, something that had happened before.

I regained control of myself and said to Dick, "I want to watch you fight for that last breath of air. You better be praying right now because you have a lot to ask forgiveness for. Do you remember Sheila Cushing?"

"Sheila Cushing? What does this have to do with Sheila Cushing? Did Weeks tell you to do this? I never told," Richard replied, visibly trembling.

"You never told what?" I sneered down at this whimpering man quivering at my feet.

"I never told anything. I need to stop the bleeding or I'll bleed to death. For God's sake, why are you doing this?"

"Sheila Cushing was my mother. I used to be named Paula Cushing, little baby Paula. Do you remember? But now I'm Karen Bickers. You killed my mother, you fucking sadist," I yelled at him.

Suddenly I heard a door open and my eyes opened wide as I saw Angela Weeks walking into the room with a large serrated kitchen knife in her hand. She shrieked, "Kill him or I will."

Richard suddenly yelled, "Angela killed your mother, not me." He looked at me pleadingly and said, "She was jealous of Sheila's attention to me. She was in love with your mother. Paula, I'm your father. I'd never have killed your mother. I loved her. We were going to get our own place."

I looked at him through this mist that was even thicker now and that sort of hovered around him. He looked pleadingly at me, then suddenly a shape started to resolve itself in the mist. It was an apparition, I guess you'd call it. It was swirling around his body fading in and out, and I could see it much clearer.

Goose bumps tingled on my arms and the hairs on the back of my neck bristled with so much electricity that they virtually crackled with excitement. The apparition was even more visible, and my breath suddenly gushed out of me as I recognized it as my mother. I knew it was her even though it was just an apparition of a skeleton that reeked of death. Putrid remains of cloth, sinews and flesh fluttered about its bones, but its ghastly presence didn't frighten me. She was shielding or caressing Dick. Her haggard bony hands with ribbons of flesh dangling from them touched his torn face. Sadness and agony seemed to emanate from the blackness of her eyeless sockets. In fact, they seemed to stare directly at me. She was real, or as real as an apparition could be. I knew Dick had been telling the truth.

While this macabre scene played out in front of me, Angela had rushed over to Richard and jumped onto his bloodied body. She immediately plunged her knife down toward his throat, but Richard moved his arm and blocked it, or maybe it was my mother who pushed the knife aside. The knife instead went through the middle of his palm, then into his shoulder. It pinned his fingerless hand to his left shoulder. Angela tried to pull it out, but it was stuck there in his shoulder.

I screamed at Angela, "Did you kill my mother?"

She made a strange sound like a horse whinny while she tried to yank out the knife, then more of her anger erupted, and it spewed out of her mouth, "He was fucking both of us and trying to take you and your mother away from me."

My mother's apparition swirled, and her phantom hands raked at Angela's face. Suddenly, Richard slammed the stump of his right hand into Angela's face and its sharp bone fragments tore into her cheek. She tumbled backward onto the floor, but quickly recovered. She stood glaring down at the evolving scene. A wicked smile spread across Angela's face, before she suddenly spat in Richard's face.

As she licked at the blood trickling onto her lips, she resumed her tirade, "He was a cheating fucking pig of a man. They both lied to me. It was his fault Sheila is dead. I loved her, but she lied to me. She deceived me and hurt me."

Angela pounced back onto Richard's stomach and smashed her fist into his face, yelling, "You know, I saved her. I took your mother in, I loved her. She was mine and he was our dick toy. Yes, your pervert of a dad was our dick toy." Richard's legs flailed about trying to find purchase to throw Angela off his body.

My mother's hands of mist pounded on Angela's body, and with each blow Angela would wince and reach about, trying to stop the attack. My mother was invisible to Angela, so she had no idea of where these blows were coming from. It was all just part of the fury of the moment we were all caught up in. Only I could see my mother's misty apparition. It was my mother protecting my Dad and bringing the truth of her own death to me.

I was stunned. What was happening was insane, and at first I didn't know what to do. Angela kept screaming things about my mother. She said, "After she had the baby, she changed. Your mother changed. She changed and hurt me. Do you understand? Do you understand, Paula?" She yelled these things without even looking at me.

"You were supposed to be my baby not Sheila's. He was supposed to make me pregnant." Just then Richard smashed his bloodied right stump into Angela's face and knocked her entirely off him again. She sprawled onto the floor next to him, then pulled back her left leg and smashed the heel of her pumps into his shoulder where the knife was embedded. The impact broke the knife's blade, and Richard, screaming in agony, pulled his hand free of his shoulder. A part of the knife's serrated blade still protruded from the back of his hand.

With cat-like agility, Angela pounced back onto him and punched him again in the face. Blood gushed from Richard's nose, but almost just as quickly he backhanded her across the neck with his hand still encumbered with the embedded knife. The serrated blade sticking out of the back of his hand sliced into Angela's throat. She reached up to stop the tide of blood that rushed forth and just then I saw through the swirling mist my mother tear open the wound even more. My mother's ashen skeletal face actually looked like it was smiling at that moment. Maybe it was.

Angela stared at me in shock as she grasped her neck with both hands, but the blood kept running out between her fingers, then suddenly she fell to the floor flailing her legs and making gasping sounds as the puddle of blood welled around her like a swallowing red ocean.

I was shocked and trembling as to what was happening. It overwhelmed me. Richard was my father, and I had been planning to kill him. I looked at his bloodied body and felt a horrible dread encompass me. The realization that I had done something so terrible made me want to vomit.

Richard spoke out in a raspy voice, "Please take me to the hospital or I'm going to bleed to death. Please help me now. Please!" Behind him hovered this apparition of my mother that beckoned me over to my bleeding father. Her face still looked like it was smiling, and I moved toward them.

My eyes filled with tears as I stood over Dick and said, "Daddy, I thought you killed mom, but it was Angela who killed her. She's evil. I'm so sorry for what I've done to you. Can you forgive me?"

To my surprise he replied, "Yes, we'll work this all out, but you need to get me to the hospital now. Call 911 and have an ambulance come."

My mind suddenly cleared, and I knew what I had to do. I looked at my father, gave him a big smile, bent over, and kissed his cheek. I could taste his blood, and it made me feel even more connected to him. I told him, "Mother will take care of you now."

I turned my head and looked at Angela lying on the floor, then suddenly heard my mother's voice deep in my consciousness telling me what to do. It had been destined all along, just as I had suspected.

I ran to the garage and opened its large doors. My life was ruined, but I had to do this one last thing. I pulled out the catapult. It rolled easily over the concrete garage floor out onto the driveway. The arm with the basket was totally depressed and ready for its load. I rushed back into the house, grabbed Angela's arm, and started pulling her over the floor. A streak of blood trailed behind her like a red wake. Daddy croaked another plea that I call 911, and I stopped for a moment and took out my phone. I called 911 and told them officer down and gave them the address.

"Daddy, they're on their way." I told him as I placed a kissed him once more. "Mother will take care of you until I finish getting rid of Angela. I love you. Please forgive me."

I dropped the phone and could hear the 911 operator still talking to me. My mother's apparition hovered over my father, brushing his hair with the gnarled bones of her once beautiful fingers. Her head was tipped low and her black eyes sockets seemed to glisten as if tears were welled up within them.

My father once more begged me not to leave him alone, but I knew mother would care for him and they needed time alone. I grabbed Angela's arm again and started pulling. I pulled her down the two steps into the garage and her body thumped down them.

The jarring suddenly brought her back to consciousness. She wasn't dead. She looked up at me and gurgled some strange sound. I couldn't tell if she was saying something or trying to breathe and it was the sound of air passing through the blood running out of her neck.

The fact that she was still alive gave me renewed strength and I pulled her quickly across the garage floor and plopped her next to the bucket of the catapult. I slapped her bloody face once to make sure she was still there. Her eyes opened and stared at me. A weird sound came from her. Probably because she could sense what was going to happen next. Then I grabbed her head and sank my teeth into her left cheek. I tore away a piece of her face and spat it into the bucket at the end of the catapult's arm. Her blood tasted sweet as it dripped off my chin. I guess if they find her body before it decomposes they will recognize the teeth marks, but I didn't care. I was fucked now and I knew it.

I hurriedly hoisted her into the catapult's bucket and slapped her a couple more times so she knew what was going to happen. I wanted to do what my Daddy had done so I took the razor and sliced deep into her stomach wall and watched as it separated and her insides spewed out into a pile of gore on top of her. A spray of bloody mist blew out from her mouth as she screamed in agony. I positioned her head so she could see her entrails slumped down onto her legs. Angela was alive enough to feel this intense pain and know that death was but minutes away. From her mouth that dripped with blood and snot came a deep groan. I watched her eyes grow larger than the full moon lighting up the Texas sky as she realized that she was about to die.

I could hear the sirens in the distance and knew my time was short. I stood next to the bucket, reached over, hit the release, and felt something slam into my body; then I was sailing through the sky in view of Angela and her trailing string of guts.

My father had built a safety bar of sort into the catapult that swung out and over the basket when the catapult was fired. It was there to insure whatever was in the catapult's basket would not fall out till its arc was completed. I had stood in its way and it had slammed me into the basket as it flung Angela's body into the heavens.

I'm now in a much nicer place where we have a club almost like the Secret Sinners Society. We get to meet and talk about things we did every week with a nice woman who loves to hear our stories. She said it's healthy to talk about these things. Every month or so my daddy comes to visit me. His hands are still a mess and I tell him how sorry I am for what I did. He says he loves me just the same, and I hope it's true. Mother visits me also, but I don't tell anyone about her anymore because they would give me some pills that prevent me from seeing her.

I like where I'm at and hope I can stay here. It's so peaceful and mentally refreshing. The place has a beautiful garden, and the buildings on the campus are Ivy League looking. Everyone is nice to me here, except that one time when an old nurse was nasty to me, but after I tore a large chunk of flesh from her arm, things have been fine. It was the same when I was in the orphanage. Some kids at first gave me shit but once I sunk my teeth into this girl's shoulder and ripped off a mouthful of her flesh, no one bothered me again. All the other kids knew that if you fuck with me, I'm going to eat a piece of you.

ABOUT THE AUTHOR

David Hearne is the author of three previous books. Two of them are political thrillers, "The Christmas Special," a novel about a Christmas morning terrorist attack on three nuclear power plants and "Hulagu's Web – The Presidential Pursuit of Senator Katherine Laforge, a story of a woman running for president. His first book was a non-fictional book titled "Enable Command Performance," the definitive guide of programming concepts.

He has also written numerous articles on technology and interviewed its luminaries like Ted Wait, the founder of Gateway 2000 Computers, Heidi Roizen, the founder of T/Maker and a former Vice President at Apple Computer.

David was a former military officer who served in Vietnam during the Tet offensive. He has two sons who have served in Iraq and Afghanistan and a daughter who is still in college.

He now lives in Southeast Texas with his wife, numerous cats at their Book Nook Inn Bed & Breakfast.

www.ingramcontent.com/pod-product-compliance
Lightning Source LLC
Chambersburg PA
CBHW030633130626
46552CB00002B/833